A Kepler's Dozen

Thirteen Stories About Distant Worlds That Really Exist

A Kepler's Dozen

Thirteen Stories About Distant Worlds That Really Exist

Edited by
Steve B. Howell &
David Lee Summers

Hadrosaur Productions, Mesilla Park, NM

A Kepler's Dozen
Hadrosaur Productions
First Edition, first printing, continuous printing on demand
First date of publication: June 2013
Editors: Steve B. Howell and David Lee Summers
Cover Art: Laura Givens

ISBN: 1-885093-68-3

Hadrosaur Productions
P.O. Box 2194
Mesilla Park, NM 88047-2194
www.hadrosaur.com

Table of Contents

1   **Introduction** by Steve B. Howell and David Lee Summers

5   **Middle Ground** by Mike Brotherton

21   **Turtle Soup** by Laura Givens

35   **The Gloom of Tartarus** by Gene Mederos

51   **A Glint off the Glass** by Rick Novy

63   **Omega Shadows** by Carol Hightshoe

77   **Daniel and the Tilmarians** by Doug Williams

101   **Exposure at 35b** by Mike Wilson

109   **Hot Pursuit** by David Lee Summers

129   **Tracking the Glints** by Anna Paradox

143   **An Eternity in Limbo** by J Alan Erwine

155   **A Mango and Two Peanuts** by Steve B. Howell

173   **The Company You Keep** by M.H. Bonham

189   **Kokyangwuti** by Melinda Moore

197   **About the Contributors**

A Kepler's Dozen

Thirteen Stories About Distant Worlds That Really Exist

Introduction
David Lee Summers and Steve B. Howell

In 1877, the orbits of Mars and Earth brought the two planets close together. The surface of Mars was mapped and its two moons were discovered. Over the course of the following decades, astronomers continued to map the red planet and discovered mountains, drifting clouds, and dust storms. They also observed what they believed to be canals and vegetation. Mars became a place in the popular imagination and writers such as H.G. Wells and Edgar Rice Burroughs imagined what it would be like to visit such an alien world.

As the nineteenth century moved into the twentieth, astronomers realized they had misinterpreted the data that led them to believe there were canals and vegetation on Mars. Nevertheless those early science fiction stories continued to inspire scientists to look for other places where life might exist. The results of those searches continued to inspire a new generation of storytellers who both imagined worlds as they might be and used those worlds as a platform to discuss issues happening right here on Earth. As the twentieth century drew to a close, astronomers discovered the first planets around other stars and finally we knew for sure there were more places in the galaxy people might imagine visiting.

In March 2009, a 1-meter telescope called Kepler was placed in orbit around the Sun. Its job is to stare at just one part of the sky and monitor over 150,000 stars continuously looking for signs of planets orbiting around other stars. As of this writing, four years after the Kepler telescope was launched, it has discovered over 2500 planet candidates and more than 100 confirmed planets.

The stars Kepler observes range in temperature, radius, and mass from about 10,000 degrees Kelvin to less than 3000 Kelvin, two and one-half times the size of our sun to 0.1 times the size, and 3 times to less than 0.05 times our suns mass. Kelvin is an absolute temperature scale used by scientists, related to the Centigrade or Celsius scale simply by being 273 degrees apart, 0 degrees C = 273 degrees K. Astronomers denote the various types of stars by a single letter designation, the more massive, hotter, larger stars being type A, the least massive, cooler, smaller stars being type M. The sequence goes A,F,G,K,M with our sun being type G, a sort of middle-of-the-road star. Distances are measured in Astronomical Units or AUs. An AU is about the distance from the Earth to the Sun, or about 93 million miles.

Our goal for this book was to bring together science fiction writers and scientists involved in the quest for exoplanets to imagine what these real places might be like. You will find stories of adventure, humor, and drama. Some of the stories are hard science fiction and others are lighter fare. In all cases, though, effort has been made to present the stories with factual information and realistic views of these real Kepler-discovered exoplanet systems. We hope these visions inspire your imagination and spark your curiosity.

The cover art shows a view of the Kepler space telescope as does the less artistic picture included on page 4. The various interesting parts are identified with the solar power collectors being the panels containing small squares on the side opposite the radiator. Inside, the telescope is the largest imaging camera ever flown into space—16 million pixels—the only instrument on the telescope and the one used to monitor all the stars.

In the book, the stories are prefaced by real scientific data for each planet and their host star. These data are presented to give the reader a feel for the type of sun and planets which exist in these alien solar systems. A few of the planets orbit two stars (a binary system) and in such cases the stars are referred to as A and B with information on both being given. The planets themselves are named, using astronomical convention, after their host star following by a lower case letter. For example the first planet orbiting a star named Kepler-15 would typically be called Kepler-15b. The next would be Kepler-15c and so on. Kepler-15a, is the star itself, and the "a" is simply never used. On the next page, we include the same data as presented for each story's alien solar system, but for our sun and three selected planets in our solar system.

Once you've acquainted yourself with the home system, turn the page and take a voyage to thirteen distant worlds that really exist...

Our Sun	Stellar Characteristics
Temperature	5778 Kelvins
Mass	1.0 Solar masses
Radius	1.0 Solar radii
Visual magnitude	-26.7
Distance from Earth	8 Light minutes

Earth	Planet Characteristics
Temperature	287 Kelvins
Mass	1.0 Earth masses
Radius	1.0 Earth radii
Orbital Period	365.25 days
Distance from Star	1.0 AUs

Neptune	Planet Characteristics
Temperature	70 Kelvins
Mass	17.1 Earth masses
Radius	3.9 Earth radii
Orbital Period	164.8 years
Distance from Star	30 AUs

Jupiter	Planet Characteristics
Temperature	165 Kelvins
Mass	317.8 Earth masses
Radius	11.2 Earth radii
Orbital Period	11.9 years
Distance from Star	5.2 AUs

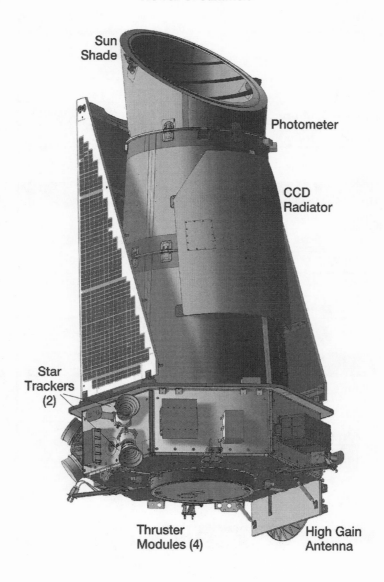

Sun Shade

Photometer

CCD Radiator

Star Trackers (2)

Thruster Modules (4)

High Gain Antenna

For more information on the NASA Kepler mission, go to http://www.nasa.gov/mission_pages/kepler/main/index.html and http://kepler.nasa.gov/.

Kepler-42

Small stars, such as Kepler-42, can have small solar systems. This very cool M type star hosts three planets in very short period orbits, the longest being only 1.8 days!

While these planets may seem far too close to their sun and far too hot to be habitable, terrestrial worlds in such tight orbits are likely to be phase-locked to their sun, the same way the moon only shows one face to the Earth. As such, the side of the planet facing Kepler-42 will be very hot, the far side very cold, with intermediate temperatures in between perhaps hospitable to a well suited human. "Middle Ground" tests our hopes and dreams related to alien life forms and brings to the fore the old adage that might makes right, or does it?

Kepler-42	Stellar Characteristics
Temperature	3068 Kelvins
Mass	0.13 Solar masses
Radius	0.17 Solar radii
Visual Magnitude	16
Distance from Earth	127 Light years

Kepler-42b	Planet Characteristics
Temperature	519 Kelvins
Mass	>2.7 Earth masses
Radius	0.78 Earth radii
Orbital Period	1.2 days
Distance from Star	0.01 AUs

Continued next page.

Kepler-42c	Planet Characteristics
Temperature	720 Kelvins
Mass	>2.1 Earth masses
Radius	0.73 Earth radii
Orbital Period	0.45 days
Distance from Star	0.006 AUs

Kepler-42d	Planet Characteristics
Temperature	450 Kelvins
Mass	>0.9 Earth masses
Radius	0.57 Earth radii
Orbital Period	1.8 days
Distance from Star	0.015 AUs

Middle Ground
Mike Brotherton

Harmony watched the humans step out of their lander, a model she hadn't seen in centuries, and into the perpetual gale of Midgard. They should have avoided setting down on plains as flat as this one and found somewhere with at least a little cover. Stumbling and hunched over, they finally managed to array themselves into a semi-circle toward nightward, avoiding facing directly into the wind.

They looked so small, their gray uniforms whipping around their unsteady bodies as they squinted to look around them. This was not a world for two legs, no aerodynamics, or a high center of gravity.

Harmony lifted herself from the ground and started forward on her six legs. "Let's go meet your true relatives, Marvel," she signed to her son beside her.

She hadn't gone more than a dozen steps when the humans started yelling and pointing excitedly. Several retreated back into the lander while others lifted what appeared to be projectile weapons and started shooting at her.

Too late, she realized her mistake. She must look a sight! A low but bulky ball of white-haired muscle, her trunk reaching forward like a menacing, grasping hand, she could not look welcoming. While she thought her tough hide might resist bullets, she could not risk her son.

"Behind me," she urged Marvel with a twitch of a thick leg. Then, switching to English, she shouted as loud as she could into the howling wind, "Don't shoot! I am Dr. Harmony Wonderkind! I'm in a native body!"

The humans stopped firing, but their weapons remained aimed at her.

Getting shot at was bad, but Harmony then wondered if she'd made an even bigger mistake. She had come trusting, and unarmed.

* * *

This business had started with the all-too-rare rainbow Marvel had spotted some months earlier. Even though Midgard had no moons, and not even night and day except as a function of location on the planet's surface, Harmony still thought in human time. The native beings she lived with and whose form she wore, twills she had dubbed them, had very different rhythms from humans, and as much as she tried, it was so hard to think like them.

On that day, although it was always day on sunside, the big infrared orb of Kepler-42 hung low in the green sky, so far nightward they had traveled. The sun was in a bright phase devoid of major spots, happily enough, as it would only continue to get colder on their pilgrimage to the geyserlands to drink, and her coat had not yet fully come in.

The tribe was grazing on ribbonwhips, a thick and meaty patch that had gotten some recent rain. She had just unearthed a plump bundle when her son sidled over to her.

Marvel excitedly gestured in the body language of the tribe and pointed nightward. "What's that in the sky?"

She shifted her focus to her nightward eyes. Dark clouds bubbled there, and before them hung the rainbow arcing across half the sky. Inside the body she now wore, the colors were odd. While she had seen many a rainbow in her long life, this was her first as a twill.

"Well, what do you see?" she asked.

"All the colors! All the twill colors, anyway. Green, then yellow, orange, red, infrared, and linfra. It's a spectrum, right?"

He had studied basic physics before they arrived on Midgard for the extended study, but Marvel had been human then, with human eyes. They hadn't yet discovered twills or programmed the xenomorph for them. "Yes. A spectrum in the sky. A rainbow is visible when there's water drops or ice in the sky splitting the sunlight into its colors. Can you see it with your human vision?"

Marvel wiggled a knee indicating displeasure. "Okay."

She switched to her human vision, too, activating her original visual cortex, which also tapped into human cone and rod cells she'd added to the natural twill eyes. The world grew darker and the alien colors faded away, while blue replaced them on the opposite side of the rainbow. It became hard to even remember what infrared and linfra even looked like, as those colors had no place in her human memory. "What do you see?"

"Home colors." And aloud in English, which he needed for words unknown to the twills, he said, "Blue. But not violet or indigo. I know it's "ROY G. BIV" for the colors, but I don't see them all."

Personally Harmony had never really made out indigo herself, but she let that part pass. "They're there, just hard to see. This sun is redder than the one our ancestors evolved under, and the human eye is not that sensitive to violet anyway."

"I prefer LIROY G.," Marv asserted, dropping the English. "Still, it's nice to look at. But what's that other thing?"

"Other thing?"

"The moving light higher up."

Then she saw it, a satellite, moving from left to right. She prepared to offer another lesson, but stopped herself. Midgard had no moons and no artificial satellites, save a set of GPS units she had deployed when they'd arrived, and their own mother ship. It had to be their mother ship, except she'd left it in a different orbit, and their ship wouldn't appear so big and bright as what she was looking at now.

Her hide rippled involuntarily with concern. "That," she said in English despite the howling wind because she needed a word, "is called a satellite."

"Oh, what's that?" Marvel asked again. "That smudge?"

This was getting ridiculous. The rainbow alone would have been a sight. Now there was a satellite and a smudge in the sky she thought might be a comet. If they'd been farther dayward they wouldn't have seen any of this. A satellite and a comet, both new in the sky. There was no way this was a coincidence.

This was a human problem, she thought. And she'd have to think like a human to deal with it, and it would take time, perhaps a lot of it. Walking back to base would take weeks. She wished she could go native all the way and stop thinking in months or days, and to stay in the moment. Thirst drove the twills nightward, and when that was slaked, they would flee the cold for desert again. Understanding their way of life and way of thinking was what her work was all about. Simple and sensible, really. She preferred these aliens to humans, at least so far. They were usually nicer, even if harder to understand.

"Marvel, we're going to have to take a trip."

"Isn't that what we're doing?"

She smiled inwardly. He was always questioning, even if he could be a smart ass. "We have to take a different trip."

* * *

Harmony and Marvel made their goodbyes, which were accepted with warmth, the same way they had originally been greeted by the tribe. The twill people were a trusting people, and dealing with their harsh and changing environment required help from each other.

Harmony worried only a little about hiking alone with Marvel, now that she knew the world better. There were predators on Midgard that could take down a lone twill, but in addition to their size, twills were smart and carried weapons. Few predators wanted to take on that combination, and Harmony had made sure that she and Marvel were especially imposing examples.

And so they traveled.

For more than two weeks they moved, Marvel in the lee of Harmony's slightly bigger body and so protected from the wind, guided by GPS implants more surely than any homing pigeon of old Earth. A new lava flow did require a three-day detour to circumnavigate, but that was not unexpected.

Sulfur smelled bad to twills, too, although bad in a different way.

Their base was sunward of where Marvel had spotted the rainbow, but knowing where to look Harmony could still make out the brightening comet, and, with the help of the schedule, the new satellite transiting across the sky.

Marvel peppered her with questions the whole way. "What's the satellite for? Is it more scientists like us? How bright will the comet get?"

She wished she knew the answers. All she could say in reply was, "Be patient. We will find out soon enough."

Finally they came to their home base. From the surface all that was visible was a camouflaged portal and radio dish emerging from a craggy outcropping. Underneath, however, existed a micromachine-constructed cavern housing their shuttlecraft and laboratory. Inside she had direct access to communications and computational power and could investigate the problem effectively, and she could leave Marvel to resume his formal lessons, too long neglected.

Before she tried to contact the newcomers in orbit, she first wanted to check a nasty suspicion. Harmony left Marvel to resume his computer-based studies (and more than occasional video games), while she contacted the mother ship. Speaking English for long stretches of time wasn't easy while a twill, but she hadn't bothered redesigning her communications interfaces for twill trunks or twill sign language. Given her trunk, keyboards were even more awkward, however.

"Sky scan for cometary transients."

"Complete. Seventeen identified."

"Give me a visual of the orbit of the brightest."

An image popped up on her display showing the sun and the orbits of the inner planets. The comet, which she'd already let Marvel name after himself, was coming in on a long elliptical. She rotated it around and would have frowned if her current anatomy had allowed.

"Give me an animated projection, compressed time step 100, including all planets on their orbits."

So there it was.

Comet Marvel was on a collision course and would impact Midgard after it swung around the sun, not very long from now at all.

It was time to talk to whoever it was in orbit. In fact, it was already late.

* * *

Being shot at was never good. Harmony realized that she should have spent more time talking with them via voice without video before demanding that they come down to Midgard, but she had been mad at them and in a fit of righteousness, cut the discussion short.

She now had a group of armed humans in her underground base and realized that if they killed her and her son, there was little she could do about it. After getting a close look at the guns, as primitive as they looked, she knew they'd penetrate her hide at close range.

Not everyone in the universe could be counted on to be fair and friendly on first meeting, and she was far from a civilized system.

Still, as long as things were framed as negotiations, she had a chance, and would try to be fair and friendly to the visitors.

"Marvel, please fabricate chairs for our guests."

"Yes, Mother."

"Thank you," said the apparent leader of the landing party. "We appreciate your hospitality and the opportunity to learn about our new homeworld."

So he'd framed the discussion, too. Fine.

He continued, "I am Commander Talbot, and I represent more than 1,000 souls on board the *Promised Land*. We are committed to establishing a colony here on the planet Freedom and Liberty, as deeded to us by the Consolidated Alliance of Planets."

Harmony had never heard of a Consolidated Alliance of Planets, but she had read academic papers about how a human diaspora into the Milky Way limited to only a fraction of light speed might lead to disjoint hegemonies. It looked like she was living the reality now.

Moreover, the better look she had of Talbot and his team of armed, uniformed, and steely-eyed men and women, the more she thought of authoritarian dictatorship.

Well, it wasn't time to fold up yet. "And I have a grant to study the ecosystem of Kepler-42d, also known as KOI 961.03, which I call Midgard, for an indefinite period of no less than a decade, from the Interstellar Science Foundation." She didn't think this would move Talbot, but it was her little attempt to claim equal credibility. Besides, she got to the planet first. Didn't "finders keepers, losers weepers" represent a more fundamental law than any established by governing bodies?

Looking at him, perhaps not.

She had also just implicitly let him know she wasn't a real threat. Maybe she had made yet another mistake. A scientist against a ship of a thousand wasn't exactly a realistic scenario. On the positive side, there would be no need for immediate violence if they did see her as a problem. What would she do? Study them to death?

"I see," he said. He turned to Marvel and said "Thank you" for a hastily supplied chair of human proportions, which he sat upon promptly.

Harmony relaxed a little more about the immediate situation, but began to feel a little helpless even though she probably weighed twenty times what Talbot did. Time to press back a little. "Surely you recognize how rare life is on planets around M dwarfs, let alone intelligent life like the twills, which I am now an example. There's so much to learn here."

"Yes, there should be value in that."

She decided to be a little more confrontational. "I'm not, how do you say, under arrest?"

He shook his head. "Hell, no, Doctor. You're just an egghead—or whatever kind of critter you are now—in the wrong place at the wrong time. We can set aside a preserve or two for your aliens, of course," said Talbot. "We'll let you stay on to help with that if you don't interfere with us. It's your only and best option."

That didn't sound like a nice option to her. "I don't think that will work. Permanent settlements in general aren't a good idea for twills, or humans for that matter, not on this planet. Tidal forces on Midgard keep it very geologically active. Also, the planet is phase-locked, and the sunside is bone dry, requiring excursions nightward for water, but it's too cold and too dark there for vegetation. The middle zones are generally unsatisfactory. And the wind ... well it doesn't ever really stop."

"Yes, I agree, it's a daunting world to settle, and you'll help us do it. You need to know that we don't have much of a choice."

"Of course you do! There are other planets in the system—"

"That are less suitable, even if they, too, weren't already spoken for." Talbot paused to let that sink in.

"Look," she said, "I don't see how you're going to manage here. Sooner or later an earthquake or a lava flow will hit your settlements. Build too far sunward and you'll have no water. Too far nightward and you'll have no light and no easy way to grow food. And the wind never stops."

"We have some ideas to tackle those problems. Wind will give us plenty of power, and we can get good at building kites," said Talbot. "And sunside isn't going to stay so dry."

"The comet," she said.

"The comet," he agreed, studying her.

Harmony thought about that some more. Her expertise was not terraforming, but she had an idea of what a cometary impact could do to a Mars-sized planet like Midgard. "Even with an impact far sunside, it's going to kill a lot of twills, either directly or indirectly, as well as disrupt the ecosystem and lead to mass extinctions, don't you think?"

Talbot actually started laughing. "Sorry, it's just that I can't believe I'm standing here having an argument with a beast as weird-looking as you look right now. It's kind of disgusting you'd do that to yourself, but your snout is just plain funny."

Several of Talbot's people snickered until he silenced them with a quick glance.

"That was unprofessional and I apologize, Dr. Harmony. Let me stick to facts. We have a responsibility to a lot of people and a plan to carry out, and a foreign scientist isn't going to stand in the way of a political necessity. This is happening."

This was not going well. "But you can't do this! These are intelligent, caring creatures that live on this world. You can't just remake their world and keep a few in a zoo, assuming they even survive what you're doing here with the comet."

"They're *aliens*, Doctor." A strange look crossed his face, like he realized he was, in effect, arguing with an alien, if not technically. "I have to put us first. You ought to realize that."

Anger flared within and she wanted to lash out, but there were a lot of weapons here and she couldn't risk Marvel's life, even if she were willing to throw hers away to hurt this arrogant creature before her. Lashing out wouldn't stop the comet, however, or the larger human threat.

Marvel asked in twill sign language, "Why did his face turn linfra?"

She replied in kind, "Because he's losing his patience, I believe. Please keep yours, Marvel."

There had to be a way to stop this. It was a tragedy on too many levels. She just felt impotent and stunned. What could she do?

She looked at him, at his face, in his eyes, and tried to

remember how to think like a human. A really selfish, ruthless human. She still didn't see any options. She needed time to think. There had to be a solution, some middle ground she could find that would make it all work.

"When does the comet hit?" she asked, even though she already knew the answer.

"About two weeks," Talbot replied in a calm tone. "I understand this is disruptive to your project here. If that's not enough time to set your affairs in order, we are capable of evacuating you and at least temporarily giving you berth with us. You'd need to get back into a human body, however you do that, to fit in our quarters, of course. You'd smell better, too."

She really didn't find the smell of twill offensive, but that was just a distraction. There was nothing she could do right now, but maybe she could still think of something. Time to appear conciliatory. "I appreciate that. It will take some time to reconstitute our human bodies, to gather my notes, samples..."

"Of course. You understand that we have to do this. There's no other option and I understand it's an inconvenience to you."

To *her*? They were doing it to a whole planet. She was glad that her form hid her emotions from him when she managed to lie, "Thank you."

* * *

It didn't help that Marvel didn't understand what was happening or why and was inconsolable when she told him that his friends might die, and even if they didn't they'd be put in jails. He had been born using her own cells and some creative genetic engineering en route to the system and had never known other humans except for herself. The twills were more normal to him.

In the meantime, Harmony remained in contact with Talbot, freely sharing data with his scientists, and appearing to be nothing else but fully cooperative. Maybe her twill biology was helping, because her human part wanted nothing more than to scream and yell and break things, and she needed to be calm to come up with a plan.

And when she tried a few experiments with her data uploads, she thought of a plan: a terrible one.

Although she did not like her idea, she decided she liked it better than Talbot's vision of the future.

She knew she should discuss it with Marvel, but was too ashamed. She just told him that she thought everything might turn out okay after all.

* * *

Almost two weeks later Harmony sat alone in her lab, having sent Marvel outside to graze. That was the right place for him at this juncture, she had decided.

She checked the clock to make sure of the time, and placed a call to Commander Talbot, eventually being put through to him. A feeling of anxious dread filled her, and it was disconcerting how much that feeling didn't seem to change between human form or twill.

She tried to ignore the dread and be optimistic. This could still end well. Before she'd even said hello, however, he was complaining to her.

"I see you've got video protocols worked out with us, but you're still a damn alien. You don't have much time to clear out."

"No, there isn't much time," she agreed. "But I have great news! I thought of a way your people can coexist with the twills!"

"Uh huh," he said guardedly. She felt like he was preparing to humor her, but ignored the feeling and pressed on.

"I will get to the point. I found the middle ground, which is really what this planet is all about anyway when you think about it."

Talbot didn't look convinced, but he didn't blow up. "Uh huh."

"It's really quite obvious," Harmony said quickly. "Terraforming, even just bringing in water, is slow. So is building settlements, especially with volcanism to worry about, let alone setting up twill preserves. Who wants to stay on a ship for years waiting? And let's face it, humans are just not well suited for this world. My idea will take a little time, too, but there's a real opportunity here for a fantastic experiment."

She paused for a breath, then forged ahead when Talbot remained silent, not even an 'uh huh.' "You can all adopt twill forms the way Marvel and I have, and live as they do, a major new nation among the peoples here. They will show you how to survive and thrive. It's really quite a nice life, in my opinion, and you can share your knowledge of science and space with the twills in exchange."

"Don't be stupid." His face practically glowed with fury, although the video feed didn't include the infrared for her to literally see the heat of it. "You've wasted my time and made us take unnecessary risks to be accommodating to you. We have no interest living like a herd of cows, or camels, or however you things live."

Talbot jabbed his finger at her. "Look at you. You're this big filthy, disgusting animal. You think we want to do that, too? No way. We're human. *We* don't change, we change the *world!*"

She let him have his moment. It was the least she could do. "I'm sorry you feel that way." And truly did feel sorry, even though it was what she had expected. "Are you absolutely sure there's no alternative."

"Yes, absolutely sure."

"We can't even talk about it?"

"No, we can't. Not at all."

It was a good thing twills couldn't cry. Harmony pressed a series of keys with her trunk.

Commander Talbot didn't strike her as the man who went around justifying his positions to anyone, but he had more to say. "Do you know why we're here trying to colonize a planet like this in orbit around such a pitiful excuse for a star? Alien lovers like you, that's why. We weren't allowed to terraform the miserable iceball we were given because of the local frost bunnies or whatever they were, and you dare offer up the same idea here? After we tried to help you?"

He leaned in. "You're just a silly scientist, playing dress up, wasting our time. The comet is on its way and we can't stop it at this point." Talbot took a deep breath and leaned back. "Look, if you elect to remain there, there's no way I can guarantee your safety."

"And I won't guarantee yours," she said, cutting off the connection.

* * *

A while later, when it was time, Harmony went outside to find Marvel.

The sun was in the same place it always was outside the base, and the wind was a terror, too, as it always was, but those things were normal and of no great concern.

She located her son grazing and moved beside him to eat part of the patch of ubergrubers he was working on, idly wondering if she should really let him do so much of the English naming of things on Midgard. Linfrared hadn't been bad, however, she had to admit...

She let herself be distracted by these small, idle thoughts for the time being. Still, Harmony was ready when the moment arrived. She lifted her trunk toward the sky. "Look up, Marvel."

The comet was alarmingly big and bright in the sky, so close it was visibly moving in real time. Also visible was a more slowly moving speck of light that was Talbot's ship of a thousand souls.

As they watched, quite suddenly and unexpected even to Harmony who had planned it, the two intersected.

Silently, an explosion of light blossomed, bright light, white light, containing all the colors of the rainbow. Harmony had to look away.

"What's that?" Marvel signed. "I don't understand, but it looks really cool."

Harmony regarded the second, temporary star in the sky. It was beautiful, but not cool at all. "Marvel, that's Talbot and the other humans and the comet has hit their ship."

"Oh," he said. After a while, he continued. "Are they dead?"

"Yes, I'm pretty sure they are."

"How come that happened?" he asked.

"I made it happen. I didn't want the comet to change things here, to hurt anyone here, or anything here to change at all."

"You told me killing was bad and I shouldn't do it."

"I know I did, and it is bad and you shouldn't do it."

"I don't believe you," he said with a strong gesture of his trunk. "You're here, they're there, and they did it by themselves because of their own mistake."

She wished that were true. How she wished. She had to be honest now with her son, however, even though she felt guilty in oh-so-many ways. "Our ancestors lived together on Earth once, Talbot's and ours, but we took different paths. Literally and figuratively. Different routes. Different planets. Different timescales. Their technology wasn't as capable as our technology." She gave him a moment to understand.

Harmony had realized that their weapons seemed dated, and that their lander looked old-fashioned, and when she'd began offering data, she'd confirmed her suspicions. Her computer could dance circles around their computer and while she couldn't be too obvious, she'd been able to control the telemetry data about the comet that it reported to Talbot and his crew. She'd used her own mother ship's interstellar drive to alter the comet's path without being noticed. Their own ship was also gone now, and they wouldn't be leaving Midgard under their own power. That was not such a great sacrifice to preserve a planet and its indigenous peoples, was it?"

"You're sure it was the right thing to do?" he asked.

Thoughtful boy, but not quite comfortable enough to be a smart aleck. Good. This was not something to joke about. "No, but it was the only thing I could do."

And as terrible as it was, what she had done, it was strangely freeing to feel such certitude about such an act. She had given them a choice, and spelling out that choice as an ultimatum would have led them to discover her deception. If Talbot had shown a spark of interest in her proposal, she would have aborted.

That's what she told herself.

"So what now?" Marvel asked.

Oh thank goodness he wasn't upset with her. She couldn't take that, even if she deserved it. "You and I go back to live with the twills and we enjoy knowing them for an indefinite time. This is our home now."

"Okay," he said. "I can live with that. I like being a twill better than human anyway. Their colors are better."

This world, Midgard, was a special place, and she was now responsible for it. She'd chosen it over her own kind, for herself and for her son.

Marvel might someday come to think of himself as a twill, good natured, in harmony with a dangerous land. Still, no matter how long they lived on Midgard as twills, no matter that she would never cry again, and no matter what the colors of the rare rainbows she saw in the sky, she had failed to find the middle ground and would have to remember one thing that would always haunt her: she was human.

Kepler-36

Here we have Kepler-36—a star with two closely spaced planets, one of which is small and likely to be a dense, hot world, possibly covered with oceans. The sun in this system slightly outshines our own, providing a nice backdrop for an amphibious tale—or is that tail? So get your mask on, your snorkel ready and sit back for a swimming good time with an adventure on the high seas with a little more gravity than expected.

Kepler-36	Stellar Characteristics
Temperature	5911 Kelvins
Mass	1.1 Solar masses
Radius	1.6 Solar radii
Visual magnitude	12
Distance from Earth	1532 Light years

Kepler-36b	Planet Characteristics
Temperature	980 Kelvins
Mass	4.5 Earth masses
Radius	1.5 Earth radii
Orbital Period	13.8 days
Distance from Star	0.12 AUs

Continued next page.

Kepler-36c	Planet Characteristics
Temperature	930 Kelvins
Mass	8.1 Earth masses
Radius	3.7 Earth radii
Orbital Period	16.2 days
Distance from Star	0.13 AUs

Turtle Soup
Laura Givens

Orrey's tentacles moved frantically, propelling her through the dark water in a tight orbit of the spacecraft.

"You're kiddin'. Zoey and fifty-four other colonists are really crammed into this fragile, little metal ball?" The thing wasn't hardly large enough to fit five Torts her size. Small as it was, it was more metal than she had ever seen in one place. Now that it had cooled enough from its plunge through the atmosphere, she wanted to see every inch of the landing pod. Two hundred and eighty-five shuttle pods had fallen all over this section of Kepler-36b but this was the pod that held her friend.

"That's what the ping address says, kiddo." Her father, Jabbo, was the chief of communications, in charge of the last cycle's worth of real-time dialogues with the colony-ship *Armstrong*. He had made his young daughter a deputy comm, after days of pleading, and assigned her to the craft's night shift. That was how she had gotten to know Zoey. For some reason, Zoey always seemed to pull graveyard comm shift. "Honey, don't get too close. If you bump that thing too hard you could breach its hull integrity. It's had a rough enough time just getting through the atmosphere. We don't need any colonists squashed like grape polyps by the water pressure, now do we?" He'd pulled a couple of strings to ensure they were both assigned to tow in the pod that Orrey's new best friend was on.

Orrey swam back to her dad's side. "Sorry, it's just so exciting. The first regular humans finally on K-36b, I can't wait to see them."

The rest of Jabbo's team moved in with nets to scoop up the pod so it could be transported to the gigantic ceramic structure known as Hab-1, docked safely out of the drop zone. For a hundred miles in every direction, crews, just like this, were ferrying other newcomer pods to their new home, the only livable place for homo sapiens on the whole planet.

"Let's just get them safely to the habitat first. There'll be plenty of time to socialize, once we make sure humans can survive in that thing. The numbers say it should work fine but the real world is the only test that counts."

Orrey rolled her eyes. She knew better than to get into an argument about the hab with her father. His design input had been voted down by the council twenty Earth years earlier and he had been grumping about it ever since. She was only sixteen Earth years old but her mother was fond of ribbing dad about the length of time he could maintain a pout when he didn't get his way. She knew Hab-1 was perfectly safe.

Orrey had seen plenty of sims of what Earth humans actually looked like and knew how delicate their physiology was. Heck that was why the Tortesie breed of human-variants existed on K-36b, to build an environmentally sound place for baselines like Zoey. Orrey's kind had been genetically engineered to withstand the crushing pressures of these oceans, but they weren't considered colonists—never had been—they'd been born here and raised by teaching machines more than thirty-five Earth years ago. No, with their turtle-like shells, enormous eyes and long, prehensile tendrils, Torts were classified as Heralds. Their job was to make way for those who were to come after.

Jabbo and his team were busy coordinating update information from the pod—there were hundreds of items to cover before it could safely dock—so Orrey, there strictly as an observer, was bored almost immediately. Since no one had actually forbidden her to do so, she tingled at the personal frequency she and Zoey had been using to communicate off-shift.

"Zoey, you in there?" she sent quietly.

"Uuuugh! Why is there an elephant on my chest?! Could someone please turn down the gravity?" A young, breathy female voice sounded tired as it tickled at her aural receiver. "Girl, that was the freakiest thing I ever want to do. I'd ask about turning around and going home, but then I'd have to go back through that goop you call an atmosphere. I looked up the crazy orbital dance this rock does with its ice giant neighbor, close as it gets, I'd at least demand dinner next time."

Orrey giggled, not a very professional response. "Don't be such a tadpole. There are double the gravity baffles once you hit the hab and I made sure to put a mint on your pillow and turn down your bedclothes."

"Now that's service."

"Watch out though, those close encounters with Kepler-36c can get everyone's hormones going."

A laugh came over Orrey's comm, then there was a moment of labored wheezing before Zoey could reply. "Ewww, the guy a couple of bunks over threw up three and a half times on the way down—don't ask—and now he just tried to scratch his nose, I think he dislocated a shoulder. What a moron."

That was what Orrey liked about Zoey, she never took anything totally seriously. It was almost like she had a Tort sense of humor. Mom said Tort humor came from the dolphin genes spliced into their matrix.

"You should have seen your splashdown from out here. There was a seismic wave that I could have surfed for miles and..."

"Look, could we continue this witty banter later? My lunch wants to come out and play." With a retching sound, the connection was cut off abruptly.

Dad was right, baselines were pretty physically fragile.

It was a good hour's swim, with the pod in tow, to the place where Hab-1 had been anchored. It was a mile-long structure that could be moved as needed, completely designed to make survival not only possible for unaltered human colonists, but downright comfortable. It was almost a self-contained world and had taken a full twenty years for the Torts to build from scratch.

Boredom soon raised its ugly head again so Orrey swam back to talk with Bimbo, a Tort who was only a few years older than her. He had pulled rear guard duty. When she was younger, she'd had quite the crush on the strapping young Tort, with his spiky shell plates and long, sinuous tentacles. He was promised to another now—*sigh*—but at least he still took her more seriously than the others did.

"Wow, is this cool, or what?" she swam rings around the young heartthrob.

Bimbo didn't smile. "Hey, Orrey. Yeah, this is pretty historic, but I'm not so sure how cool this will be for us."

"What are you talking about? As of today, K-36b is a full-fledged colony world. We're citizens, you big goof."

Bimbo looked around and set his comm-caster to mute. He motioned for her to do the same.

"Did it ever occur to you that now that real human's are here, we're just going to become second-class freaks? To them we aren't real people at all. Sure, we get a block vote when it comes to policy, but when you read the fine print, the base-lines can veto anything we propose. I've heard rumors, that on other worlds, the Heralds die out as a species within a few generations of baseline colonization. Really, it's easy enough to do, just slip in an expiration date when you design the species."

Orrey was stunned. She'd heard, and ignored, such bilge over the last year but she'd never expected to hear crap like this coming from Bimbo.

"That's crazy. Colonists couldn't survive five minutes on K-36b without us. I just talked to my friend, Zoey, and they're helpless as tads in a trim-tank."

Bimbo snorted and pointed several tendrils at the pod they were following, "Friend, that's a good one. Are you going out reef-hopping with her this weekend? Sharing a polyp salad? Hell, no. Once they're safe in the habitat that we built for them, the only use they'll have for us is as janitors and repairmen. Maybe they'll let us run errands for them. You've read Earth history, we're just the happy little darkies on this plantation."

"What a hateful thing to say!" She slapped at Bimbo's eyes. How could she have once liked him? He turned and grabbed at her flailing tendrils.

"Grow up! In their eyes we're monsters, leviathans of the deep, bred and domesticated for their needs. Educator drones taught us to think like humans, and yeah, ninety-two percent of our DNA is human, but an Earth chimp has a higher percentage in common with homo sapiens than we do."

Orrey shook herself free and sped off from the tiny convoy. She didn't even want to share the same ocean with Mr. Bimbo Haley right at that moment. This was supposed to be the best day ever and now it was ruined.

* * *

She swam for several minutes till she was sure she was out of comm range. Who was going to miss her anyway? Off in the distance ahead she saw another pod being ferried to

Habitat One, Probably the delta four team. She hid in a reef of pseudo-coral rather than explain why she was out wandering around so far from her own assigned group, during the biggest event in K-36b history.

It couldn't be true, she told herself. *Humans weren't like that, certainly Zoey wasn't like that.* Maybe she should swim back and see if Zoey felt like talking. Bimbo was a creep for spreading such vicious lies.

She hung behind the spiked growth, miserably watching as the other convoy made its way past. It was sure to be a mad-house once all these pods started docking with the habitat. She shouldn't just stay hiding here like a cowfish while there was so much work to be done.

In the distance, moving toward the delta four convoy, was a shrikefish, a true leviathan. These bad boys were five times larger than a full-grown Tort and covered with sharp-toothed, articulated mouths that fed on everything in their path, sending all that food to the great central stomach it dragged in its wake. In the early days, these monsters had been the bane of Tort existence, but once a sub-sonic frequency was found that repelled them, they weren't much of a threat at all. This one was a biggie, and was getting closer than she'd ever seen. Usually they would zoom off once they got in range of the sub-sonics, but this one was just putting on more speed.

"Hey!" she literally screamed into comm-set, "Crank up your sub-sonics. That shrike isn't slowing down!" She knew she was casting on the right frequency but all she heard in reply were frantic orders and the sounds of panic. Before she could even register a response, the shrikefish gobbled up the hindmost Tort. The others quickly turned to face the menace, but their gigging spears and plasma shells were no match for all those mouths. The defenders were all gone in under a minute and the great fish began gnawing at the floundering shuttle pod.

Orrey stared in wide-eyed horror as the thing's teeth scraped along the metal hull. It was strong, but after its plunge through K-36b's corrosive atmosphere, and the splashdown impact, the hull integrity had to be badly compromised. After a few moments of frustrated chewing, the shrikefish wheeled around and slammed its enormous gut into the metal sphere.

What happened next was horrible. The pod ruptured and started to explode, but the pressure of the waters around them reversed things almost immediately and the ball twisted in on itself. The implosion compacted everything that had been a part of it, or lived within it. All that was left was a small mangled hunk of meat and scrap metal, barely an appetizer for the ravaging giant.

Oh god, oh god, oh god! She turned and fled, desperate to get back to her father's team. It was at least a couple of minutes, at her top swim speed, before she was in comm range. The shrike was already on her tail, but at a distance. At least her sub-sonics seemed to be keeping it at bay.

All those colonists, dead! Thoughts kept ringing in her head. *Trillions of miles to be snack food for a monster.* She'd known a couple of the Torts in that group. *Why hadn't the sub-sonics worked?* On the contrary, they had almost acted like a dinner bell.

"Orrey Salinas to convoy delta six, come in. Emergency! I repeat, emergency!" She prayed she was close enough to be heard, the monster was still on her tail.

"Orrey, Honey, what's the matter? Where are you?" Her dad's voice sounded frantic.

"There's an insane shrikefish headed right for you. It destroyed delta four—Torts, colonists and everything. Dad it's after me, coming right your way." She was already exhausted, terrified and out of her mind with worry. "Daddy, what should I do?"

"Veer off, kiddo." Jabbo's voice sounded strained. "There's a megalith forest ten degrees south. If you can make that, you'll be safe till I can come get you."

"Okay." She replied weakly and flicked all her tendrils into the water at once, executing a perfect ten-degree turn. Orrey put everything she had into speed, not letting herself dwell on what would happen in she didn't make it. After a few seconds, she finally dared to glance behind her. The fish wasn't there. It had streaked on, ignoring her and making straight for dad, Bimbo, and Zoey.

"Dad, it didn't follow me. Get out of there!" Once again the dinner-bell image struck her, the shrike seemed so focused on getting to that colony pod. *Oh crap*! "Listen, I think the shuttle is putting out something that cancels the sub-sonics and actually attracts shrikefish."

There was a long pause. Orrey wondered if her dad thought she had cracked up.

"Honey, I want you to keep heading for that forest. You understand? I can't just leave these people." Another pause, "I love you, baby." And the comm went dead.

She didn't even stop to think, but lit off after the receding shrike. Screw the forest, her father and friends were in danger.

* * *

With a speed she didn't think was in her, she caught the creature, or at least its bulbous stomach. Her plan, such as it was, involved using her gigging spear to slice open a hole in the thing's gut and shove in all the plasma shells she had. At best this might give the damned fish a stomachache bad enough to stop his attack. At worst it would annoy Mr. Shrike and make him chase her instead, once she turned off her sub-sonics.

The third scenario hadn't even occurred to her. Orrey's spear broke with her first stroke, and the shrikefish didn't even notice.

She could just make out Zoey's pod in the distance ahead, floating free. Had her dad abandoned them?

Her private comm tingled. "Orrey? What the hell is going on out there? The crew is trying to shut down all the systems, but they keep injuring themselves getting to the controls. Morons! Did they not read the instruction about staying in their couches? No one will tell us anything!" Orrey had never heard such a panicky edge in Zoey's voice before.

"There's a humungous shrikefish out here that wants to eat the pod, or at least crush it. We think something that the pod is broadcasting is attracting it."

"W-w-what?!"

"I don't see dad or any of the others, but I'm coming. Hold on, I'll find some way to stop it." Orrey did not say this last part with much confidence, but it just had to be true.

"No! No you will not." All panic and false levity was gone from Zoey's voice. "I just looked up shrikefish on my pad and you have zero chance against something like that. I think the other Torts had the right idea and I order you to get the hell out of here too."

Suddenly, out of a patch of stew-weed, four Tortesie streaked, each holding a corner of the net that had been used to haul the Earth pod. Within seconds ten more followed, whooping and taunting the shrike. More than half the shrike-fish's lethal mouths were caught in the net's tough filaments as the first four sped through the deadly maws in a corkscrew pattern. The rest were harassing the thing, though their weapons had little real effect.

Orrey laughed out loud. This was Tortesie humor at its finest.

"Hey Zoey, You remember how you were trying to explain cowboy movies to me? I think the cavalry just arrived." With a flick of tentacles, she propelled herself into the fray.

The thing about shrikes that always baffled the Torts, way back when, was their lack of sensory apparatus. No eyes, ears, noses or manipulators to touch with. Just all those mouths. Turns out their eyes and ears were in their mouths. Dad had told her that when she was six, and it looked like he remembered now as well.

Spears, tipped with primed plasma shells, stabbed into mouths causing some actual damage to the thing. Orrey followed suit and attached a shell to what was left of her spear and made for the nearest mouth. The mouth had seemed to have a life of its own, bobbing and weaving. Several times, it was a close thing whether the mouth would bite her before she could feed it a plasma lozenge, but she eventually did and it made a satisfying sizzle as slime drooled out of the orifice.

In the middle of her victory dance, she felt sharp pain in three of her dorsal tentacles. Another mouth had grabbed her when she was distracted. It didn't bite through the appendages but held her tight so it could drag her toward its other waiting maws. A spear tip sliced into the mouth and it let go abruptly. She turned and wrapped her injured tendrils around her savior.

"Dad! I thought you'd died or run off."

Her father held Orrey tight for a few seconds before releasing her. "If we live through this, you are so grounded."

"We're going to beat this thing, right?" There was more pleading in her voice than she would have liked.

"If I had fifty Tort marines and a few bazookas ... maybe." He swam with her away from the battle, toward the still floundering pod. "Look, all my comm gear got smashed by the shrike so I need you to contact your pal, Zoey, on that personal frequency you two cooked up, and see if they still have any form of propulsion that works. The further away they can get, the better their chances of survival." She could see Bimbo, part of his shell crushed in, waiting for them. "We're going to hold laughing boy off as long as we can, but I want you two to get this thing moving any way you can. Understood?"

They both said their *Yes, Sirs* but Jabbo had already turned back to the fight.

Bimbo winced, "I checked the whole pod out and I think there are a couple of places strong enough to hold up under some nudging. That's the best plan I have."

Orrey nodded curtly. "Okay, let me call Zoey, like dad said, see if they've got anything."

Suddenly her comm came to life and she realized Zoey had probably been listening all this time.

"Okay, I asked the captain already and he said these things weren't paddleboats—his words, not mine—about all there is might be the auxiliary retro pack, if it didn't get burned up. It wasn't used during descent but if we fire it down here, it'll probably just punch right through us. Sorry, Orrey."

Bimbo had switched personal comm frequencies and was listening in. what more was there to say, so they shared a miserable moment of silence. Then, all at the same time, three voices broke the stillness in unison. "I just had a really stupid idea."

* * *

"Yeah, Cap says you're hovering right over it. It's the red packet."

Bimbo's tendrils twitched in frustration. "In this light, everything is shades of grey, don't they teach you anything in Earth schools?"

"Bite me, turtle boy!"

"Can we focus here?" Bimbo and Zoey had known each

other for two minutes and already they were arguing like an old married couple. Orrey could see that the struggle with the shrike still continued and it was closer than before. There were five Torts floating, unmoving, in the water. The net was shredded in more places than she could count. What good was a stupid plan if no one was left to watch it fail.

"Okay, the captain says it should have a big triangle on it and say something like 'Danger, this thing will kill your ass.' I'm paraphrasing, of course." It sounded like Zoey was beginning to warm to her new role as liaison.

"Got it!" Carefully they undid the fasteners and slid the retro rocket out of its casing. "So, how do we detonate this thing?" Orrey found two metal tabs that had to be contacts.

Zoey breathed a labored sigh over the comm. "That part had the captain stumped, but I might have a thought on the subject. One of you takes your comm receiver and attaches it to the two leads you see. Then, when one of you shoves the rocket up that thing's ass, the other one yells something nasty, a tiny charge goes through the receiver, boom."

Orrey and Bimbo exchanged a look. "Well, other than a shrikefish not actually having an ass, per se, I like it." Bimbo started to remove his commset.

Orrey grabbed it from him. "With your shell all banged up, you don't have the speed, but you still have strength and can get the pod far enough away to maybe minimize damage to it. I'll do my own yelling too, if you don't mind. I know lots of nasty words."

He stared into her eyes.

"Shut up. You know I'm right."

Zoey's voice spoke up, "Damn it Orrey, I don't…"

"You shut up too! This round's on me and that's all there is to it." She took the comm and stuck it on the improvised bomb. "Bimbo, toss out a scatter signal and get pushing." She didn't look back to see if he'd done what she said but soon there was a shriek sounding through the water that every Tort knew the meaning of.

As she zipped toward the monster, the Torts broke off what they were doing, grabbed fallen comrades and lit out in every direction. They may not know why the scatter signal had been triggered but their response was trained in from childhood. The shrike struggled to free itself from what was left of the net. At the last moment she changed trajectory so she would miss all the snapping mouths and come up on the thing from behind.

It was a shame she couldn't say some brave last words to Zoey, to pass on to her father, but she was afraid it might set off the retro before she was ready. She knew that, not only was. there not a convenient anal opening, but the way the fish was thrashing, she was going to have to hold it in place herself to make sure it did its work.

Through tears, she searched for a likely spot on the swollen gut of the creature. Then she noticed something odd. There seemed to be something leaking out of the disgusting gut, not much, but noticeable. It was hard to see with all the move- ment, but there it was. Her little gigging spear had done more damage than she had thought. She slipped two small tendrils into the hole—*yuck*—and pulled as hard as she could. The fish jerked and the retro pack went flying. *NO!*

But a tentacle was there to catch it.

"Not only are you grounded, no allowance for three weeks." Her father grabbed one side of the tiny rip and Orrey grabbed the other. Soon the fissure was big enough and Jabbo slammed the rocket pack deep into the thing's stomach. "I don't know what the plan is here, kiddo, but I bet it's a doozy. We good to go now?"

Orrey nodded and they were off.

Fifty yards, a hundred and suddenly a triumphant squeal erupted from dozens of mouths and she knew the shrikefish was free. She redoubled her efforts and screamed into her comm microphone. "DIE, Motherf…!"

The ocean behind her became a solid thump, which sent her reeling. Her last memory before the blackness closed in was of a great gout of meat bouncing off her shell.

* * *

It was weeks before Orrey got the complete story on what had happened. What was attracting the shrikefish turned out to be its signal beacon, set to a very low frequency to travel further in the oceans of K-36b. It was an unused frequency, chosen completely at random. Eight other convoys had been attacked, three of those survived the engagement, though none as ingeniously as the Delta Six team had.

"I look like a freak." Orrey wiggled the mechanical tentacles that replaced the ones bitten, and infected by the shrikefish. Her father had shielded her from a lot of the blast that killed the shrike. He was still in intensive care, but doctors said he'd be okay.

"Gripe, gripe, gripe! You are such a wuss." The hologram of Dr. Zoey Graves examined the area where she had attached the prosthesis tendrils to her friend's ruined ones. "I don't hear Bimbo complaining about the shell-cast I put him into."

"That's just because he's all relieved to hear that he won't have to learn *Camptown Races* on the banjo." Orrey slid out of the med bay, kind of an oversized drive-through CAT scanner hooked to the outer hull of Hab-1. Zoey's holo-face looked puzzled. Orrey laughed "Oh, you know, order 7-C, the one that makes us full fledged citizens. He was sure you guys were coming down with whips and chains."

Zoey's image enlarged till it was about the same size as Orrey. "Yeah, well, that wasn't so far off with the first couple of Earth colonies and I was shocked 7-C hadn't already been implemented here. Bureaucratic morons. Fortunately, we humans learn from our mistakes eventually. Baseline human doesn't mean much these days." She blinked all four of her eyes and rubbed her bald head.

'We humans', Orrey liked the sound of that. She had already decided she would be the captain of the first Tortesie star ship. There were a lot of planets out there for 'we humans' to explore.

Kepler-34

Ah ! I hate the thought of aliens inside me… Oh wait, I should begin with the facts. Kepler-34, a binary star consisting of two sun-like companions, is the host to a long orbital period, pretty big planet. The planet orbits in the habitable zone, which means liquid water could exist on its surface. The problem here is that Kepler-34b is unlikely to have a solid surface. But large planets often have large moons, and their surface is another story all together. Nothing like a habitable moon to allow a civilization to flourish, or at least give it a try.

Kepler-34 A,B	Stellar Characteristics
Temperature	5913 / 5867 Kelvins
Mass	1.0 / 1.0 Solar masses
Radius	1.2 / 1.0 Solar radii
Visual magnitude	15
Distance from Earth	4887 Light years
Orbital Period	28 days

Kepler-34b	Planet Characteristics
Temperature	340 Kelvins
Mass	70 Earth masses
Radius	8.6 Earth radii
Orbital Period	289 days
Distance from Star	1.1 AUs

The Gloom of Tartarus
Gene Mederos

Mother had gone into labor in the middle of the sleep cycle, which Dano took as a sign that his little brother would be something of a nuisance for the rest of his life. He could tell by the anxious looks on the adults' faces that something was going wrong in the delivery room. He couldn't help but wonder, in the morbid fascination of the very young, if his sibling to be hadn't been eaten and replaced by a cuckoo. Everyone knew the story of the first woman who had gotten pregnant on Tartarus. A cuckoo micro-spore had burrowed its way inside her, attached itself to the baby growing there and started to feed. When she finally went into labor, the human baby had been all eaten up and a baby cuckoo had slithered out of her and skittered away.

Eventually, Nela the nurse came out of the delivery room, holding his father lightly by the arm and guiding him out of the waiting area. All the faces in the room turned to follow them, and Dano figured most of them had wanted to ask what had gone wrong, but none of them did. And something was definitely wrong, for Dano had never seen his father look so scared, not even that one time when a swarm of burrowers had tried to get through the plaz window of their home.

It seemed like an eternity to Dano, and he would never have admitted he had started to worry about his mother and the baby both, before Doc Schoen finally emerged from the delivery room carrying a plaz box, readouts flashing on its transparent surface. All the adults gathered around to peer into it and it was then that Dano figured out that his baby brother or sister was probably inside. One of his uncles noticed him standing there and made way for him to approach. He was suddenly really scared that maybe there was a cuckoo inside the box, but he screwed up his courage, as his father had taught him, and looked inside. The baby looked fine to him, and he exhaled in such obvious relief that a few of the adults couldn't help but smile.

"Say hello to your little brother," Dr. Schoen said through

his respirator, which made his voice sound strange, but Dano knew the doctor couldn't breathe their air and had to wear the respirator outside his home and office.

"Hello Miko," Dano said, reaching out his hand to touch the box. "Why is he in there?""

"Ah," the doctor said, looking around at the adult faces, some of who nodded for him to continue. "Your brother was born without the adaptations the Company engineered into your ancestors." Dano knew that the 'company' was responsible for their being on this world and that the company had been punished, but somehow, his ancestors hadn't been able to leave to find a better place. Unless...

"Does that mean he has to leave?"

"Yes, I'm afraid so," replied the doctor, "your brother was born with the Pardon."

Many of the women started sniffling and a few of the men shook their heads, everyone looked sad. They waited until Dano's father returned then offered their condolences. They asked about his mother and father told them she was doing as well as could be expected. He knelt down in front of Dano and told him so himself.

"Your mother is fine. She and the baby will rest here tonight and we'll come see them after breakfast." His father put his hand on his shoulder and took him home.

* * *

Back in his office, free of the respirator and rubbing at the spots on his jaw where it chaffed, Dr. Schoen called up a 3D display of their world, the only moon of the planet Kepler-34b, a circumbinary world orbiting its two suns in the constellation Cygnus. To the human eye, in the color-corrected light of the telemetry images, the moon had appeared made of pastel hues of robin's egg blue, blushing pink, gold, sunsets and lavender, all swirled together like a child's finger painting. Initial data from the probes sent to scan the world showed an effusive, overwhelming propensity for life. The gaseous Saturn-sized planet the moon orbited sat along the inner edge of its star's habitable zone making the moon, sweltering in its almost perpetual shadows, just the right temperature for certain kinds of life, life that flourished in hot, wet darkness. The world had been named Darwin, in unabashed optimism of the sheer wealth of life, and the corollary monetary riches that predicted. Now Darwin Station had sole claim to the name, the inhabitants having christened the planet one of the many names in classical literature for hell.

Not that there was much reading of literature, classical or otherwise on Tartarus, Dr. Schoen reflected. He himself had a few ink printed paper books, moderately priced antiques in the rest of human space, prized possessions here where the local micro-fauna included intractable life-forms that devoured anything organic.

But he was safe from all the spores and microorganisms that abounded on this world here in his hermetically sealed habitat, which included his office and a small living area and lavatory. A living area he now shared with a newborn baby, for like him, the baby could not survive the world outside his self-sterilizing airlock without protection.

He stared blankly at the holoscreen generated by the comm unit. He was required by law to inform the medical authorities about the birth, but he was very tired. It had been a trying and protracted delivery. With a sigh, he turned off the comm unit and went to bed.

The next morning the father and the six-year old arrived early. Dano kept yawning and rubbing his eyes but was obviously happy to see his mother, and quite intrigued by the baby in the box. Dr. Schoen observed them from behind the glass that separated his office from the examining room. The parents took turns sliding their hands into the steri-glove inserts to caress their son. Each time they did so a smile would leap to their lips and just as quickly vanish as they realized that he would soon be taken from them. He could see that Dano had begun to notice the changes in their expressions. Eventually the boy started turning and glaring at him whenever either of his parent's sighed. A bright lad, he knew it would be the doctor that sent his brother away.

It was much later in the day, after the family had left, that Dr. Schoen finally made his decision to rebel and carry through his plan. It wasn't fear of winning the enmity of a six year old nor guilt at causing grief to the parents that decided him. No, it was, that at heart, he was a malcontent. Wasn't that why, after all his fruitless little attempts at rebellion, they had sent him to this hellhole?

Dano's father returned to see his wife and child after dinner. Dr. Schoen asked him on the comm to join him in the consulting room where he and his patients, or their loved ones, could sit comfortably across from one another, separated by an almost invisible electrostatic screen. It was much more personable than speaking through glass.

"I'll come right to the point Jarret, I think I can avoid sending Miko away."

"What do you mean? Surely you're not suggesting that we modify him." The technology was available, for Dr. Schoen was a geneticist, and an avid researcher of the genetic engineering that had been used to modify the original colonists. But the look of horror on Jarret's face reminded the doctor of how deeply the aversion to genetic tinkering ran on this world. To the colonists it wasn't just illegal, it was anathema. Jarret would never consider it, even if it allowed him to keep his newborn son. The doctor sighed.

"Of course not," he reassured the anxious father. "Even though those microbes that live in your blood in benign symbiosis with you, that allow you to thrive out there, would devour a human, such as myself, or your son, who hasn't been adapted to host them, from the inside out. Fortunately, the adaptations were designed to develop during the fetus' growth, so the company genegineers didn't alter the ability of the placenta barrier in your women to screen out microbes. You all actually acquire your lifelong guest as you take your first breaths of this world's spore-laden air. Miko has not been exposed to them yet."

Dr. Schoen leaned back in his chair.

"Those microbes are a blessing to you all here, but a terrifying curse to the rest of humanity. They are so virulent, that if a single creature escaped your body it could wipe out all non-fungoid life on a world."

"Which is why we are never allowed ascent from Tartarus." Jarret stated flatly, not allowing any emotion in his voice.

"Unless, like your son, one is born without the adaptations, is never exposed to the world's air, and is bundled away in a hermetically sealed plaz pod and shot up to the station with the monthly harvests."

"But how do we keep it hidden?"

"From whom?" The doctor waved his hand idly to indicate the entirety of the small human population outside. "You're the colony administrator, the only one who ever has a reason to talk with the people on the station. Call everyone who was here last night and tell them I erred, that Miko has just enough of the adaptations to make him unwelcome on the station but not enough to survive without a steri-suit. They may not all believe you, but nobody in this colony would ever betray you to the authorities."

"Won't he have to live here, with you?"

"Not at all. I'll requisition another hermetically sealed unit, tell them I'm tired of living in such cramped quarters and want to add another room," the doctor smiled wryly, "a reading room. You can attach it to your home instead."

The doctor knew that nobody would be concerned about the cost of shuttling the unit down from the station, the pharmaceuticals that were developed from the harvests of Tartarus had made the colony very prosperous, with precious little to spend its money on.

"But if it the secret gets out, won't you be punished?" Jarret inquired carefully.

"They sent me here for my past sins, what more can they do to me?"

* * *

Dano waited impatiently for Miko to catch up, more annoyed than usual at the inconveniences the little sporling caused him on a daily basis. Of course, Dano was unaware that a great deal of his annoyance and frustration sprang from the fact that he had fully crossed over into adulthood and had an important job as a hauler pilot, while his brother still lagged just on the other side of puberty. And still his parents insisted that he look after him, an insult to his burgeoning adult pride. Now, the lagging part he definitely understood; although the plaz steri-skin his brother wore to protect him from the world's microorganisms was supposedly impenetrable, he had been taught since infancy to walk through the world with especial care. This exaggerated care made him slow, and it seemed to Dano that he was forever waiting on his brother.

Dano sighed in exasperation, he was hungry and wanted to get home for the midday meal. Like the rest of the colonists, he knew what day was, he'd seen 3D holovids of other worlds and even Earth that were lit by a warm, but not too hot sun. There was no day whatsoever on Tartarus. The small moon orbited its huge planet in a special and rare synchronicity that kept it in shadows, shielded from the twin stars of the system. Occasionally, one might see a painfully bright crescent in the sky, which illuminated the world in a strange half-light that distorted the shadows, but mostly the gloom of Tartarus was relieved only by starlight on clear cloudless nights, which were rare, and the steady beacon that was Darwin Station in geosynchronous orbit above the colony.

It wasn't that far a walk from the school complex to his home. The entire colony fit snugly inside a crater, where a meteor had struck the moon some millions of years ago. The crater had been chosen to establish the human colony because it was in the moon's 'arctic' region, which was slightly cooler and drier than the rest of the world. The habitats inside the crater were the best that money could buy. The colonists had big, largely unspent, bank accounts up on the station. His parents' unit was no larger or smaller than the rest. His father didn't enjoy special privileges for running the colony.

The kitchen table was set lengthwise against the observation window of Miko's room. Father sat on one end and his mother Elan, a comp-tech by trade, on the other. Dano sat facing his brother through the glass. Bowls of steaming stew occupied their attention, and there was very little conversation as they ate in a comfortable silence. Until mother glanced through the window at her younger son.

"Aren't you going to finish your lunch?" she asked Miko.

Miko had pushed back from the bowl of stew. He'd eaten about half of its contents, various fungi, algae and roots in a thick creamy broth that was extracted from a parasitical air plant. Like everything mother prepared, it was traditional and delicious. Dano had often wondered if it tasted the same to Miko as it did to them. His food had to pass through the steri-unit built into the wall to zap anything microscopic and living that might hurt him.

"I want to pack it up and finish it on the flight, I've never eaten on a hauler before." Miko beamed at his older brother.

Dano tried not to let the surprise and irritation show on his face. He had totally forgotten he was supposed to take his brother with him on the afternoon flight to collect the harvesters. He had made other plans, plans that would now have to be changed. Mother was smiling at Miko's enthusiasm, but father was looking right at him. Dano knew better than to break a promise to Miko. He allowed himself a grimace.

"You will not touch anything aboard the hauler with sticky fingers. Understand?"

The airfield lay just outside the crater that housed the colony. Fortunately for Dano's frayed patience, a transport tube ran through the wall of the crater to the airfield beyond. They exited the shuttle just a few dozen yards from the aircraft. It wasn't a sleek machine, the hauler; basically a large square cargo hold where plaz containers of raw organic materials and the smaller harvester units that gathered the stuff could be secured while flown from the fields to the plant. Four lift units and a bubble-shaped cockpit were grafted on in a most ungainly fashion. But it could fly, and Dano liked nothing better than to fly.

He keyed in the coordinates for the first harvester team and plotted in the course so it would be registered with the air traffic control comps, as per the regs. Then he keyed in the ignition code. He couldn't help but smile at this younger brother as the craft thrummed to life and the controls lit up beneath his hands. They lifted above the glittering lights of the colony, always shining against the darkness, a beacon to all the colony's ships. But as beautiful a sight as that was, he always lifted his eyes to the stars. The hauler's cockpit bubble canopy allowed him an expansive view of the heavens, and even though the craft's flight ceiling didn't really bring him any closer to them in any significant way, he felt closest to the stars when he was in the air.

All too soon, he was landing the craft so the first harvester team, four rovers with multiple waldoes and attachments waiting next to a number of containers they had filled with raw organic materials that would be processed at the plant into the compounds the pharmaceutical companies on the other human worlds could make into medicines and health products. As he dropped gently into the field covered by rubbery semi-spherical growths, one of the units waved an arm at him. He smiled. That would be Arisa. He ignored his younger brother, who had seen the smile and was smirking.

The cargo hatch dropped open, becoming a ramp so the harvesters could roll into the hold and load it with the containers. Once all the containers were onboard, the harvesters themselves latched onto the sides of the hauler and Dano lifted the whole ungainly construct into the air and flew them all back to the plant. He picked up three other teams the same way. After dropping off the last team, he flew a short distance away from the plant and settled the hauler in a hollow of multi-frond pseudo-algae that waved gently in the air currents. He turned on all the hauler's lights to full intensity. The fronds ranged in color from a deep lavender to a bright gold so the scene was very picturesque. And waiting amidst the fronds, not far from where the hauler had landed, was Arisa, the lights of the hauler picking out the gold highlights in her hair. Most of the other harvester personnel took a much more comfortable transport back to the colony, but Dano was always glad that Arisa preferred to ride back with him.

"Stay here," he ordered his brother.

"Aye, Captain," Miko said jauntily.

Dano opened the smaller passenger hatch behind the cockpit and stepped down into the field to meet her halfway. He knew how much Arisa liked romance. She had chosen to meet him in this field because it was so pretty, and while he himself didn't care a whit where they met, or how, he knew what she expected of him. He would take her in his arms and kiss her amid the fronds. But he hadn't taken more than a few steps before he felt a short sharp jab of pain in his thigh.

Catching himself before he could slap the source of the pain away, he flipped on his palm-light and examined the long spiny thorn embedded in his leg. Had he slapped it, another spine would have embedded itself in his hand. The ends of the spines protruding from his leg were already engorging themselves with his blood.

"I'll get it Dano!" Miko said, dropping down from the hatch behind him.

"I can get it," he growled. He didn't really have any cause to be angry with his brother. He'd walked too close to a dart nest, hidden among the fronds, and disturbed the air around it, setting it off. Fortunately all but one of the spray had missed. Miko stepped forward anyway, setting off another small spray of darts in his direction. Two struck him and bounced off the plaz-skin of his steri-suit, dropping impotently at his feet.

"Miko, get back before you get me punctured again." He reached into the pouch at his belt and withdrew the cryosprayer. A single short burst would have sufficed to kill the thing and dislodge it from his flesh, but he was still angry, so he sprayed it with LN_2 until the dart shattered into ice crystals. Like most of the fungoids found on Tartarus, the dart carried a mycotoxin, but it was one humans had built a suitable immunity to thanks to the symbiotic microorganisms in their blood. All he'd get was a mild, barely itchy rash. The sudden realization that the same toxin would have paralyzed his brother and stopped his heart sobered him immediately.

"You okay?" Arisa asked, with just enough concern to show she cared without making him feel foolish for having tripped the dart nest.

"I'm fine," he said, smiling.

"Hey, shrink wrap." She greeted Miko with a warm smile. "No dart nests in the direction of the plant, at least I didn't trip any, but we'd better get inside."

Dano and Arisa settled into the comfy overstuffed flight chairs in the cockpit. Dano turned to Miko, who was strapping himself into the auxiliary seat behind them.

"Hey squirt, the hauler felt a little sluggish on the landing, why don't you step outside and check for damage to the lifters? Since you're armored against darts and all."

Miko grinned to let his brother know he understood and would take his time checking the lifters.

Dano was rather engrossed in Arisa when the first few frilly half-moon shapes struck the cockpit window. The feeling of revulsion was instantaneous. A burrower! He imagined he could hear the spit-sizzle of its organic acids as it attempted to eat through the plaz. Arisa gave a small scream. He realized his brother was in danger a split second before he heard his quivering voice on the comm.

"Dano...? Dano...? Burrowers everywhere..."

And then his brother screamed.

"I'm coming, Miko!"

Without stopping to suit himself up, Dano popped the emergency cockpit hatch, Arisa handing him his survival belt, and dropped outside. The lethally dangerous macro-spores, one of the most intractable banes of the colonists, wafted about on the air currents, resembling nothing any more dangerous than sets of human eyelashes.

Dano ducked and weaved as he made his way down the length of the hauler. Where the hell had Miko got to? He felt the first fiery, incredible painful sting on his shoulder. It made him reel. Even the thickest plaz would eventually melt under the highly corrosive excretion. He had no choice but to duck under the craft to avoid a small clump of the things floating towards his face. He gritted his teeth as he fumbled in his pouch for the neutralizer, fighting the pain as the acid ate through his flesh. He sprayed the foam from the canister on this shoulder. The needs of the colonist to protect themselves on such a hostile world had spurred great advances in biochemical and molecular science. The foam not only neutralized the acid, it rendered the burrower inert and alleviated quite a bit of the pain.

"*DANO!*" Miko wailed in his ear.

"Get under the hauler!" Dano yelled back. And back towards the tail assembly, caught in the light between the landing struts, a small, writhing shape rolled under the craft. Dano crawled towards him, his brother crying piteously in his ear. He could see immediately where the burrowers were eating through the plaz of the steri-suit, he could smell the acid burning his brother's flesh. Taking a deep breath to steady himself, Dano began to apply the neutralizer. He treated two spots on his brother's legs, one each on his arm and torso, and then flipped him over to treat the five incursions on his back. Then gathering his brother in his arms, he ducked out from under the hauler and ran as fast as he could for the hatch.

One more got him, in the small of the back as he entered the craft, but Arisa was there with the neutralizer from her own belt kit. Dano lay his brother down on the seat Arisa tipped back for him. The boy was whimpering a little, but he was trying to be brave. Then Dano looked on in horror as a slew of purple spots began to cross his face, his eyelids swelling blue. Something in the air had already gotten to his brother. Even now any of the many voracious microorganisms infesting the world could have entered his body through his eyes, nose or mouth. Dano strapped himself into the pilot's seat and hurried through the ignition sequence. Arisa moaned somewhere behind him and his blood ran cold.

"His eyes just rolled up into his head." Arisa was crying. "Oh Dano, there's something a lot like a rotter breaking through the skin on his cheek."

Dano swore and didn't bother to lift to cruising height before leaning on the throttle.

"Is the respirator still functioning?" Dano asked suddenly.

"Yes he's breathing, but it doesn't sound right."

Dano tried to remember what it was he'd once heard about rotters affecting the respirators of the early colonists, but it had been generations since rotters had been of any concern to humans. Then it hit him, warm moist air, CO_2.

"Use a touch of cryosparay on the respirator, just in case something wants to grow in there and choke him."

If Dano had been impatient with the world before, it felt nothing like the sense of urgency and dread driving him now. He flew right over the airfield and landed right in the square in front of the medical center, ignoring the squawks of the air traffic control comp. Arisa had called Dr. Schoen on the comm and so the doctor had cycled the airlock and was waiting just beyond it when Dano entered carrying his brother in his arms. A gurney waited in the airlock and Dano gently lay his brother on it.

Jarret and Elan arrived within minutes and the entire family waited anxiously while Dr. Schoen worked frantically over Miko's body. After a very long hour, the doctor came out to see them.

"He has a few really bad burns, but Dano neutralized the acid before it could reach the bone. He's inhaled a few spores, at least one is a mild hallucinogenic and another appears to be having a soporific effect on him so it's all to the good."

"All to the good?" Jarret looked confused. "What about the other spores? The ones we've been shielding him from his whole life!"

"Can you arrest them, before they kill him?" Elan asked in fear.

"His body has already done so. And it looks like he will heal up quite nicely."

"How is that possible?" Dano thought to ask.

Doc Schoen sighed and sunk into a chair. He rubbed again at the spots on his temple where the respirator still chafed. After all these years he had still not found one he could wear comfortably. "I suppose I should tell you the whole truth."

"What truth?" Jarret said, with some suspicion.

"Your son was born with the Pardon, but that wasn't all he was born with."

"What are you talking about?"

"I ran the first genetic essay of your son when I was examining your wife, at the start of the second trimester."

"You what?" Jarret looked as shocked as his wife.

"I knew then he would be born with the Pardon, and an idea occurred to me."

"You had no right!' Elan said.

"No. I suppose not. But it was an opportunity I couldn't pass up."

"What opportunity?" Her voice rose even higher in anger.

"Being born with the Pardon doesn't mean one is born without the engineered gene sequences that allow you all to live here, only that they are not expressed. The way the company genegineers designed it, a single amino acid in the hemoglobin molecule is added to switch on the adaptations. This is why we get a child born with the Pardon every few generations; the amino acid is not created. Your son did not have it. I knew that with a few modifications…"

Both mother and father launched themselves toward the glass that separated them from Schoen.

"You altered our son?!" The father yelled in obvious horror.

"No!" Dr. Schoen actually stepped back away from the glass in the face of the parents' fury. "I knew you all would tear me apart with your own hands. Believe me, I know how deeply wronged you all feel. I modified some of the microbes that I had managed to extract from Elan's blood. I altered them so they would pass the placental barrier and enter your son's bloodstream, but I weakened them to near somnolence. In effect, it was like the live vaccine technique pioneered in the twentieth century."

"That's why he was so sick as a child, the fevers, the upset stomachs..." Elan could barely hold back tears, and the doctor was sure they were equal parts rage and grief.

"You told us it was a buildup of his own bacteria in the habitat. That we had to keep replacing the air scrubbers..." Jarret slapped his hand against the glass and turned away from the doctor.

"I'm telling you the truth now."

They had all turned away from him, so Dr. Schoen went into the exam room. When he returned he was leading Miko by the arm, now free of the steri-suit, wearing only a hospital gown and a respirator, for his lungs would still have trouble with the world's air. He appeared weak, but steady, his arms where they showed beneath the gown covered here and there with a diagnostic patch. Schoen walked him over to the airlock. Everyone looked on in fear and anticipation as it cycled. And then Miko stepped through and was gathered up in his father's arms, and his mother's, and finally, his brother's, who held him gingerly as if afraid he might break.

Dr. Schoen left them alone for a good long while. Then he cleared his throat.

"If you can stand to part from him, he should now be sent up to the station to see the doctors there. They'll have to call in immunology specialists from one of the more advanced worlds, but I believe that by examining Miko, they can make a vaccine to protect the rest of humanity from your deadly little symbiotic friends."

Miko spoke up first.

"And once everyone on the station is vaccinated, Dano can

be allowed to fly the shuttles up and back?"

"And I believe that someday, he or you or some other hell-spawn not yet born, will be able to visit the other worlds of humanity."

Miko looked up at his father and mother in turn. Then he looked at Arisa, who was looking at his brother, a shy half smile on her face at the look of hopeful anticipation she saw there. Miko smiled at his brother.

"I want to go, I want Dano to fly to the stars," he said, and he knew in his heart that it would be so.

Kepler-3

A nearby cool K-type star plays host to a mini-Neptune like planet. The short 5 day orbital period causes the planet's atmosphere to be extremely hot, far above that which we take as a habitable temperature, in fact about the melting point of Plutonium. However, the planet and its magnetic fields, reaching to and interconnecting with its host sun, make for a great scientific laboratory—or do they? Ya just gotta go wid the flo, mon.

Kepler-3	Stellar Characteristics
Temperature	4780 Kelvins
Mass	0.81 Solar masses
Radius	0.75 Solar radii
Visual magnitude	9
Distance from Earth	124 Light years

Kepler-3b	Planet Characteristics
Temperature	878 Kelvins
Mass	26 Earth masses
Radius	5 Earth radii
Orbital Period	4.9 days
Distance from Star	0.05 AUs

A Glint off the Glass
Rick Novy

As soon as the door closed, claustrophobic pangs began. How many times had Dabrina done this in practice, in simulators, and in drills? Those could never be the same as the real deal. The planet, formally known as Kepler-3b, with its funky magnetic field and proximity to its star—nothing could have prepared her for the reality of this moment.

"What's the matter, Dabrina? Your pulse is up."

Leron's smooth but decidedly Jamaican accent calmed her, at least a little bit. She pictured his square jaw and dark complexion as she took a deep breath. "It's just nerves, I guess."

"You're doing fine. Just memba to breathe."

Doing fine. She hadn't even released the docking arm yet, and already her heart did a drum roll. What would it be like out there, really out there in that magnetic field? She took a deep breath, and it seemed to help.

After going through the end of the checklist, the time had come. "Request permission to release the arm."

"You ah go."

Dabrina released the clamp holding her pod to the arm. That little action gave the pod enough momentum to drift clear of the mothership. Dabrina scrambled to get the pod turned about so she could get the mission underway, forgetting all about the nerves she had a moment ago.

"You away. Go catch that tendril. See if you can learn something about those crazy readings we saw."

"Thanks, Leron. See you in a few hours." She checked the magnetometer, watching the digits rise as she entered the magnetic field of the planet Leron had named simply Wicked. An appropriate name it was, too.

There would be no colony here. Too close to the star, as uninhabitable as Venus in terms of temperature, but that wasn't the worst of it. Wicked's sun boasted a powerful magnetic field that interacted with an unusually strong magnetic field from the planet on a regular basis. That caused all sorts of havoc in the form of ionizing radiation and showers of subatomic particles.

No, colonization would never happen on Wicked. Scientific investigation was another matter, just not an easy one.

Part of the problem with magnetic fields is you can't see them with your eyes. You can only see their effects. In the case of the tendril currently joining the star and the planet, all Dabrina could see was a pinkish glow, presumably from charged particles corkscrewing their way along the magnetic field lines. Subtle, yet beautiful. She would have to take care not to allow it to become hypnotic.

As she got closer to the tendril, the magnetic induction drive became more efficient, and she found herself accelerating toward the faint glow of the tendril. Not that it was outside the plan, of course. That had been intended all along, and then the plan meant to try corkscrewing around the entire tendril to collect readings with the magnetometer, spectrometer, mass spectrometer, Geiger counter, and dozens of other instruments all running in concert. It was a simple job, at least in theory.

In practice, Dabrina never did have complete faith in these induction pods. They worked fine in Earth's magnetic field, even during heavy Val Allen Belt activity. Out here, this application was completely untested. She glanced at the pressure reading on the emergency hydrazine thruster for comfort, then had her focus torn away when Leron called over the radio.

"How is she handling?"

Dabrina had to confess she hadn't had any of the problems she imagined. "Good, so far."

"Just hold to the plan, mon."

She had to laugh despite herself, and thanked the stars that Leron made the mission, and not Elliott Krantz. She didn't even want to think about working with that man. Elliott Krantz, with the knot in his underpants. "I'm holding to the plan, man."

"You still don't say it right."

"You can try to teach me when I get back."

"You got a deal, mon."

After putting the radio back into monitor mode, she got ready for the corkscrew insertion maneuver. The hull of the pod would be charged, and travel along the tendril in much the same way as a particle traveled along a magnetic field line, only on a much larger scale. So long as the tendril held its integrity, the mission should be a slam-dunk.

As far as Dabrina could tell, the flux lines were indeed tightening, but not quickly. Thinking nothing more of it, she activated the trajectory in the computer. The magnetic induction drive felt nothing like the chemical rockets more commonly used. The gradual inductive acceleration did not approach the three to four gees from those.

A superconducting coil, a burst of current, and steering plates to direct the resulting field to interact with the field from the planet, and away she went. While the acceleration was less, she could keep it going for far longer than most other engines, taking most of the energy from the planet's magnetic field itself.

A quick pass through all the state-of-health screens on the computer said she could relax for a while, so she simply looked at the pink streamer leading from the star to the planet, where it merged and blended with the atmosphere.

After a while, even looking at that became old, so she checked the timer. Still an hour before the main maneuver. It would be all action then, but for now, she decided to try to rest. Dabrina leaned back in her couch and slowly closed her eyes. As she did, something yellow darted past the window. Her eyes snapped open, but whatever she saw was no longer there.

It must have been a glint off the glass. She tried to rest again, even closed her eyes for a spell, but simply had too much mission adrenaline in her veins to fully relax. Relaxation wouldn't come. Instead, she simply stared at the tendril, its pink swath growing ever larger, its growth unnoticed by the second, but clear by the minute.

As time dragged onward, Dabrina found herself looking for that yellow flash again. Her eyes tended toward the spot on the glass where the glint originally appeared, trying to will it back into being. Just a glint off the glass? She knew it had to be something more.

When the maneuver began, it caught Dabrina by surprise. The sudden change in momentum jarred her from the trancelike state of thought she had been in. Not much later, the radio came alive with Leron's voice. The sound quality had degraded significantly since the last contact. Interference from the close proximity to bizarre magnetic fields of the tendril, no doubt.

This might be the last contact until after the mission ended.

"We are detecting several anomalous—" A crackling hiss replaced Leron's voice. She never heard the end of the thought.

"You're breaking up, Leron. I didn't catch all of what you said."

More hissing responded, so Dabrina had to assume he could still receive her signal. "—several anomalous magnetic—" More hissing.

She shook her head, although she knew nobody could see it. She had to assume she was on her own. "Leron, you're breaking up. I'll watch for magnetic anomalies. See you on the other side."

"—near your trajec—" Hissing static, and then, "—detecting large fluctuations in—" Even the bits she understood were buried in static.

"Leron, your signal is down in the mud. Wish me luck." With that, she would still listen, but there was no sense in fighting a losing battle. She could still feel the gentle maneuvering of the spacecraft as it guided itself to a path parallel with the magnetic tendril.

The maneuvering had been programmed, but charging the hull to allow the magnetic field to take over, that task had to be initiated manually. It was a safety precaution to allow safe abortion of the mission for reasons too intangible or subtle to leave to a computer to decide.

Times like this, when the computer held her life in its hands, she felt the most anxiety. She could suppress it enough to get through the training and the boards and the psycho-analyses necessary to qualify for the mission, but reality always trumped training. She thought about a computer with hands, and it made her smile as she wondered if programmers could ever make a computer understand the inexact nature of human speech and idiom.

The beeping of an alarm brought her back to the task at hand. Ninety second countdown alarm. When it reached zero, the pre-planned time to charge the hull would arrive. So far, all systems were go. She waited for the timer to reach zero and then initiated the charge. Immediately, she felt the pod begin its spiral around the magnetic field lines.

One of the reasons Dabrina had been selected for this mission was her seeming immunity to motion sickness, and she sure needed that now. The pod whipped around the tendril fast enough to cause gees to change more intensely than the steepest rollercoaster she had ever tried. In a controlled situation, she might even enjoy this ride. Here, she knew the potential dangers all too well.

The magnetometers and electric field meters collected data far too fast for human eyes to follow. There would be plenty of time to review the results later. For now, her job consisted of waiting to blow the hydrazine thrusters to eject herself from this berserker path before she got too close to the Wicked's atmosphere. The only other task not assigned to the computer was the release of dyes into the environment, but she wanted to wait until the onboard equipment had collected at least ten minutes worth of benchmark data before altering the environment.

After all this time spiraling, Dabrina thought she could see a hint of yellow—the same color as the glint off the glass she saw earlier as she approached the tendril. There seemed to be more than one, but whenever she leaned toward the glass to get a better look, they vanished from view. Perhaps they trailed the pod and only came into view unintentionally. Regardless, it convinced her that something was out there.

After a while, it became a game to her. The glints would appear at the edge of the glass, and she would try to catch more than a glimpse of them. Occasionally, she could briefly make out what looked like a spherical collection of sparks or electric discharges in yellow, but the opportunity to observe them never lasted more than a fraction of a second.

Another burst of static came from the radio, but nothing intelligible came through. Dabrina gave a half-hearted reply, but she knew the tendril had complete control of the radio spectrum in this part of town. Still another burst of static, but this time she didn't bother to attempt an answer. While she wondered about the message, she tried not to let it worry her.

Perhaps she should have. Almost immediately, the pod encountered unexpected turbulence, throwing Dabrina into the sidewall of the gee-couch. She thanked the stars she remained strapped in or she might have broken an arm. What had just happened?

While the buffeting continued, she did regain enough composure to check the magnetometer only to discover the readings all over and changing rapidly. Only one situation could explain these readings—the tendril would snap soon.

Another violent thrust, this time from straight ahead, pressing her hard into the belt. It hurt, and the buffeting grew still more extreme. She had to get out, had to abort. Dabrina extended the joystick with the controls to fire the hydrazine thruster and minimally steer the pod under thrust. A twitch of a thumb and she felt her body pressed against the couch. A split second later, the most violent buffeting of the journey began, allowing very little control over the pod.

Shaking from left to right, then up and down, and at the same time, spinning and spiraling, Dabrina felt the purest form of terror she had ever experienced. Just when she thought it would never end, it did. The hydrazine tank exhausted itself, and the pod became still. Out the window, she saw nothing but a faint pink glow coming from all around. She knew where she was—the worst place possible to be—inside the tendril.

Time to regain composure. Time to think things through. If the magnetic field lines twisted to the point the tendril snapped, who knew where she might end up—thrown into Wicked's atmosphere, pulled into the star, or most likely, destroyed by the unleashed raw energy.

It should be easy enough to use the magnetic induction drive to kick herself out of the tendril. She powered up the coils, but nothing happened. Not good. Without the induction drive, she would be completely at the mercy of the magnetic fields. That fate, Dabrina did not trust a bit.

She started a diagnostic at the same time she tried again to initiate the induction drive, but that produced the same nothing. A moment later, the results of the diagnostic displayed on the screen. Magnetic induction drive inoperable. No kidding. The question remained, could it be fixed, and quickly?

She queried the computer for more detail and a screen of text followed. Burned out induction coils. That was one repair she couldn't make without some facilities, not that she would even consider getting out of the pod to try. That metal ball afforded at least some minimal protection as a Faraday cage, protection that she would no doubt need.

The pod settled into what seemed to be the center of the tendril, and everything became still. Too still, like the calm before the storm, or the eye of a hurricane. The stillness made the hair on the back of Dabrina's neck stand up, and her chest curdle with anxiety. She couldn't help but feel totally helpless.

Even if the coils were useless, the instruments were not. The magnetometer kept recording data all along. Maybe Leron and the rest of the crew could recover the pod and learn all the secrets this place held. Duty didn't soothe her anxiety, nor did it settle her mood. It had to be done, but then, not much else could be done at the moment. Out the window, she could see only a faint pink glow from all directions. Over the radio, inevitable static. She saw no sign of the yellow glints she had seen just moments before encountering the turbulence.

It seemed all that remained to do for this mission was wait to die. How long would it take to exhaust the air? Would it last longer than the power supply? Inside the magnetic field, everything depended upon those induction coils; they generated electricity when not being used for locomotion. Even the air scrubbers relied upon their power.

Or, perhaps Leron would send the utility shuttle after her. She knew that was not an option. Inside this tendril, the trapped plasma would charge the hull faster than turning on a light bulb, and the utility shuttle had no mechanisms in place to deal with that problem. No, here inside this unique occurrence of the galaxy, this tendril so odd and rare it attracted aliens from many light years away, she was completely and utterly alone.

She noticed her hands trembling and willed them to stop. She ran diagnostics again, wishing for a different result she knew would never come up. And then, the fun began.

At first, the vibrations remained almost imperceptible, barely registering on the magnetometer, much less physical sensation. All at once, the magnetometer showed over-range, and the turbulence began in earnest. It shook the pod without mercy. This time, Dabrina knew there was no recourse but prayer, and to all the Gods from every religion.

With the magnetometer useless, and the electric field meter not much better, Dabrina knew what must be happening. The tendril had twisted, and rupture would occur soon. Although the buffeting made concentration difficult, she tried to keep her eyes on what was outside her window. It had started as a faint pink from all directions. Now, the pink had gained energy, radiating with maddening ferocity. Along the twisting tendril, she could see a faint patch of yellow much more vast and pale than the glints Dabrina had encountered earlier.

No, this light differed from those elusive spheres of wonder. This, like a stroke of white-hot flame injected along the tendril from the star, or from the planet. She knew not which, as she had no way to take her bearings without use of the magnetometer. Dabrina realized this brightness closed in distance, and would be upon her in an instant.

* * *

Glittering stars filled the view from the window of the pod. In the distance, a trio of glinting yellow spheres danced an intricate tango. Dabrina turned her head to compensate for the pod's slight rotation. The glints off the glass. They were real; she hadn't been imagining things.

As the pod turned, Wicked came into view, beautiful with its red land beneath cyan-tinged white clouds so alien to look upon. She could find no trace of the tendril or the faint pinkish glow she had grown so accustomed to seeing. She patiently waited for the pod to rotate the planet out of her field of view replaced again by the starry skies of Kepler-3b. But this time, something looked out of place.

Dabrina leaned closer to the window and focused on a spot an undetermined distance from the pod. There, in the blackness of space, she could see hundreds upon hundreds of tiny yellow sparks, orders of magnitude smaller than the glints, and all dancing an intricate tango to an unseen band. At that moment, she heard Leron's voice over the radio.

"Dabrina, do you hear me? You okay, mon?"

The dancing sparks had so mesmerized her that she could not pull herself away from this spectacle. Leron repeated his message.

"Dabrina, do you hear me?"

This time, she pulled her attention away from the window long enough to activate the microphone. "I'm here, Leron."

"The tendril snapped. We thought we had lost you, but I found the pod with the sixteen-inch telescope. There you were, surrounded by balls of yellow light." Leron paused a moment, but the pause gave Dabrina no words to describe what she had just witnessed.

His voice came over the radio again. "What just happened out there, mon?"

"A miracle. Or maybe two."

Kepler-30

Three planets grace this sun-like star, two more-or-less like Jupiter with one being a Neptune-like planet. The two inner planets would be pretty hot worlds while the outer planet is of a temperate nature and, if a large moon were present, might have a good potential to host life. Prepare for intrigue and mystery as you ride along on this thought provoking and mind-bending story where the good guys and the bad guys often get mixed up.

Kepler-30	Stellar Characteristics
Temperature	5498 Kelvins
Mass	0.99 Solar masses
Radius	0.95 Solar radii
Visual magnitude	15
Distance from Earth	4564 Light years

Kepler-30b	Planet Characteristics
Temperature	548 Kelvins
Mass	>60 Earth masses
Radius	3.7 Earth radii
Orbital Period	29 days
Distance from Star	0.18 AUs

Continued next page.

Kepler-30c	Planet Characteristics
Temperature	431 Kelvins
Mass	>75 Earth masses
Radius	14.4 Earth radii
Orbital Period	60 days
Distance from Star	0.30 AUs

Kepler-30d	Planet Characteristics
Temperature	323 Kelvins
Mass	>65 Earth masses
Radius	10.7 Earth radii
Orbital Period	143 days
Distance from Star	0.5 AUs

Omega Shadows
Carol Hightshoe

Selaynia crouched in the shadows of the landing deck and watched as Mallory and the security detail walked around the battered black shuttle that had been brought to Melpomene. She stifled a laugh as one of the men poked at the hand-held sensor then shook his head.

"No readings, Commander," he said shaking the device.

Of course not. That's an Omega shuttle, Selaynia thought.

:Mallory is concerned it might be a Confederation trap, Smokeshadow said.

Selaynia rubbed the silver wolf's ears. The female wolf had been with her almost a year since the wolf's previous partner Jaharel had been killed. She glanced over at the other wolf with her, a silver-tipped black wolf who had been her partner for several years. Shadowmist was watching the group closely and she knew he was working to make sure the three of them remained undetected.

Selaynia waited until the group finally left the landing deck. "Anything?" she asked.

Smokeshadow bobbed her head. *:The shuttle was found drifting just inside the second asteroid belt. Mallory is concerned it was placed there by the Confederation.* The wolf paused, her head cocked to the side and her ears forward. *:Two of the guards are being stationed outside. Mallory apparently doesn't want anyone to know about this.*

"He's worried. We're hearing more rumors the Confederation knows where we are, and the last couple of raids that went out were attacked before they hit their targets." Selaynia kept her voice low as she spoke to the wolves. She might not be able to speak mind-to-mind with them, but they had better hearing than she did and they were very intuitive.

She had been angry with Mallory ordering her off the landing deck when she arrived. She was a former Omega operative who had defected to the Confederation during the war and she knew Mallory still didn't fully trust her since she had no way of proving she had defected on orders from the Alliance. Despite the work she had done for him and the other leaders of the growing rebellion against the Confederation, he kept her out the loop on anything sensitive. Having picked up a battered Omega shuttle in the Corycian System would be something sensitive.

Still, she was an Omega operative and this was an Omega shuttle. She wasn't going to let Mallory keep her away from it.

:The guards outside are getting bored and their attention is wavering, Shadowmist said standing up.

Selaynia stood and brushed her long silver hair back over her shoulders then headed for the shuttle.

The black shuttle was battered, but she didn't see anything that resembled combat damage. Melpomene Mining Station in the Corycian system was a place that before the war had been avoided by all but the mining groups. Frequent plasma storms and three asteroid belts made for a dangerous trip to reach the inner planets and their moons.

She found herself just staring at the shuttle. She had not heard any rumors of any Omega operatives that might have survived the end of the war. When the Confederation set up their occupation of Alliance planets they executed as many members of the Alliance government and military as they could capture. They had given no quarter to those on the battlefield even after the Alliance's surrender.

Selaynia ran her hand along the side of the battered shuttle. She stopped, her hand resting on the Omega emblem on the door. "This was Nolan's shuttle," she whispered.

She leaned against the shuttle, unable to stop the images that flooded her mind. Standing in the shadows behind the security chief of Athena Station Twelve, waiting for Admiral Ganelon and his detail. Her hands clenched tightly as she remembered recognizing Nolan as the person she had been required to kill to prove to the Confederation she really was a traitor to the Alliance. She had only hesitated a few seconds before pulling the trigger on her mentor and Omega's director.

:Stop thinking about what happened the last time you saw Nolan. You know he survived that incident and he agreed with your actions. Shadowmist's voice pushed the images out of her mind as he nipped at her ear.

Selaynia looked up and shook her head. "Yes, I know that, but it still bothers me that I was able to pull the trigger on Nolan that easily."

:Easy? Selaynia that wasn't easy—if you hadn't finally pulled the trigger when you did, McKeon would have seen you. You hesitated too long in taking that shot and you know it. Now, stop this and get inside that shuttle.

Selaynia stiffened at the harsh tone in the wolf's voice.

She frowned as she looked again at the Omega symbol. Most of the shuttles worked on either voice recognition or a remote door system to prevent them from being accessed by unauthorized personnel.

She placed her hand over the symbol. "Selaynia," she said.

"Code name?" The voice was Nolan's and Selaynia shivered.

"Silver Shadow." Her voice was barely louder than a whisper.

The door opened and Selaynia had to pause as both wolves boarded the shuttle in front of her. Their noses were up as they sniffed the air. She felt the light mental probing from both of them as they searched for anyone who might be hidden on the shuttle. Her hand went to her dagger as she waited on the wolves to finish their search.

:Clear, Shadowmist said.

Selaynia stepped into the shuttle cautiously. There were protections Omega used that would not have reacted to the wolves, but would react to a humanoid presence in the shuttle. She spun around as the door closed behind her and slammed her hand against the control panel. Nothing happened—the shuttle was sealed.

"Okay Nolan, what's going on?"

"You gave the code name of Silver Shadow." The recorded voice paused then started again. "I had heard you were on Melpomene and hoped the shuttle would make it there."

Selaynia settled into the pilot's seat as the recording continued. Based on the requirement for a code name, Nolan had probably recorded several different messages depending on who found the shuttle.

"I have begun gathering all of the operatives I can locate

as well as other trusted members of the Alliance on one of the moons of Kepler-30d."

Selaynia was out of the chair and back at the door as the shuttle began powering up the engines. She hit the control panel several times, with no results. "Nolan!"

She pulled a dagger from her belt and used it to force the panel cover open. The dagger fell to the floor with a clear ring of metal on metal as a shock went through her hand.

Shadowmist and Smokeshadow's howls echoed in the small shuttle. Selaynia dropped to her knees as the wolves howls grew louder and was joined by a shrill loud siren from the shuttle computer. A hissing sound came from the vent and Selaynia held her breath as she forced herself back to her feet and started working with the door controls.

Another electrical shock dropped her back to the floor as the shuttle continued to fill with gas. "Shadow? Smoke?"

Both of the Canthralian wolves were unconscious, but she could see they were still breathing. "Nolan...." Her voice trailed off as darkness descended.

* * *

Selaynia woke to one of the wolves licking her right cheek. "What happened? How long?"

:*Some type of knock out gas,* Smokeshadow said.

:*Unknown how long, but we are away from Melpomene and the shuttle has landed,* Shadowmist said.

"Landed?" Selaynia stood up and grabbed the wall as a wave of dizziness hit her.

Her energy pistol was in her hand as the door to the shuttle opened.

:*It's Nolan and McKeon,* Shadowmist said.

"Announce us," Selaynia whispered.

Shadowmist positioned himself next to the door and growled loudly.

"Selaynia?" A voice called from outside.

"Nolan? If you are Conrad Nolan—what is my code name?"

"Silver Shadow and the furball."

:*I hate that nickname!* Shadowmist launched himself from the shuttle.

"Selaynia call you partner off!"

"Shadow." Selaynia stepped out of the shuttle with Smoke-shadow next to her.

"Welcome to Omega Shadows." Conrad Nolan stood up and held a hand out to Selaynia.

She paused and studied the men in front of her. Conrad Nolan was a few inches taller than she was with dark brown eyes and hair now streaked with gray. His face had more lines and there was a new scar on his neck. The other man, Bobby McKeon, still looked much like the last time she had seen him on Athena Station Twelve. His dark blue eyes seemed to hold more sadness than she remembered, but there was still a glint of humor in them.

"Nolan...." She stopped as the memory hit her—Nolan's body dropping to the deck of Athena Station Twelve after she shot him.

"You followed orders and did what I expected." Nolan pulled his hand back and continued to watch her. "However, I am grateful Shadowmist was able to warn me about what was coming."

Selaynia only nodded, not trusting her voice at that moment, and looked around. The shuttle had landed in an open area, but she could see this was a world not too unlike Wyvern, and that sent a warning signal through her. Omega Shadows, as Nolan had called it, was warmer than Wyvern and felt more humid. "Where are we?"

"Omega Shadows is a moon of Kepler-30d," McKeon said.

"Just how long were we unconscious?"

"Better you don't know," Nolan said. "Come on, let's get you some food and fill you in on what's going on."

Selaynia followed the two men back to a group of small buildings, Shadowmist and Smokeshadow next to her.

:I'm sensing a number of familiar minds. Shadowmist paused. :And something else. It's like there is another group here but not here.

:I'm sensing it too, Smokeshadow said. :Almost as if something is watching us.

"What's going on?" Selaynia asked.

"Inside," Nolan said.

From the outside, the building had looked like the normal, drop-in-place, quick-set-up temporary building most of the Alliance military used. Inside they were in even rougher shape than she would have thought.

"Nolan, Shadow sensed something out there, like something was watching us. What is going on here?"

Nolan motioned to a small table in the far corner.

"I've been trying to gather as many people as I can and bring them here. I don't know what the presence is that Shadowmist sensed, but it is strong enough that even the latent telepaths I have found can sense it."

"And...." Selaynia paused. "Look I know Mallory hasn't been able to do that much against the Confederation. He's dealing with more and more refugees that aren't fighters. But if you're looking to establish a base to hit the Confederation from, why not work with him? The mining station on Melpomene is already established and has resources."

"We're looking for something else," McKeon said. "We're looking for a place to bring the refugees and establish a world without the Confederation." McKeon paused. "We had heard you were on Melpomene and with most of the telepaths in the Alliance having been slaughtered by the Confederation, we needed to get you here."

"Or at least get the furball here," Nolan said.

Shadowmist growled.

"However we didn't know a second Canthralian Wolf was with you." Nolan held his hand down for Smokeshadow to sniff.

"This is Smokeshadow. She was Jaharel's partner."

"Jaharel? Wasn't he—" Nolan stopped.

"Yes. Don't ask."

Nolan only nodded. "That presence was why I sent the shuttle. I know Mallory is concerned about Confederation spies on Melpomene—that's the reason for abducting you like I did."

"It almost didn't work. Mallory didn't want to let me anywhere near that shuttle. He still doesn't trust me. He still sees me as a probable traitor to the Alliance."

"I'm not surprised and I'm sorry that's where you ended up when you got away from Wyvern."

"So you sent the shuttle specifically because you wanted to bring me and Shadowmist here—so what's really going on?

Stop playing the Omega games and tell me straight up what I'm doing here."

"The Confederation avoids this system. We don't know why, but we suspect it has something to do with the telepathic field Shadowmist and I'm assuming Smokeshadow sensed," Nolan said. "Other than the Rhiash, we are not aware of any other telepathic races within the Confederation and they wiped out the known races within the Alliance. With the exception of the Canthralian Wolves."

"The Wyverns are the dominant race within the Confederation," Selaynia said. "And they seem to be psy dead. Other telepaths have problems reading or projecting to them."

:What we are sensing seems to be slightly different from what we consider normal telepathy, Shadowmist said. *:If Wyverns can feel this presence the same way Smoke and I can, then they may be avoiding this system because of that. However, unless there is something else preventing them from coming here, then I doubt it will keep them away if you establish an Alliance colony here.*

"That's what I thought," McKeon said.

"That's why I needed you here," Nolan said. "We need someone to try and find out what this is and if possible contact it. We need a safe place for people to come and start rebuilding."

"But without knowing what this is, you don't know if this will remain a safe location." Selaynia stood up. "Okay, I'm willing to try and locate whatever it is Shadow and Smoke are sensing. But first I need to get some real rest. I will also need all the information you have on this planet and system."

"Come on, I'll show you the shoebox you'll be using as quarters." McKeon stood up and gestured to the door.

"I'm not sure how long Nolan has been here," McKeon said. "I've been here for about four months myself and most of the other Omega people were already here. I arrived much the same way you did. An Omega shuttle and a cryptic message from Nolan."

"How does he know where anyone is?"

"I haven't figured that out. But it seems like he gets a premonition or something and sends one of the shuttles off. It usually returns a few days to a several weeks later with someone."

They stopped in front of one of the smaller buildings. A one-person shelter was all it really was. McKeon opened the door. "It's got a cot, a food station and a computer interface—that's about it."

"It'll do." She laughed as both wolves jumped on the cot. "Although if I can get a second cot for me, since the four-feets seemed to have claimed that one, I would appreciate it."

"I think that can be arranged."

Selaynia put a hand out. "How is he, really? Something doesn't feel right."

"I'm not sure. There is something different about him, but I can't figure out what. It's just a feeling."

"Maybe it's just the circumstances."

"Maybe. I'll be back in a few minutes."

Selaynia watched him walk back to the main group of buildings, then turned back to the two wolves.

"Any comments?"

:*There is something different about Nolan*, Shadowmist said. :*I'm sensing something lost in him. I think it's more like he's trying to refocus and find a new purpose now that Omega no longer exists.*

:*It's tied to the presence we're sensing*, Smokeshadow said.

Selaynia looked at the female wolf and raised an eyebrow. "Explain."

:*Every time I try to read Nolan, I get a sense of that same presence wrapped around his. Almost as if it is cloaking him somehow. I'm not getting it from your other friend or anyone else—just Nolan.*

:*Smokeshadow is more sensitive than I am at this type of reading*, Shadowmist said.

"Okay so another reason to see if we can locate this un-known presence. Do you two think we can do that or at least find a way to contact it?"

:*Only if it is willing to let us.*

"You two get some rest. I'm going to review the informa-tion in the computer and see if I can figure something out."

The door to the shelter opened and Selaynia barely stopped herself for throwing the dagger that was in her hand. "McKe-on, you really should have knocked first."

"Sorry. I was trying to knock and the door opened." He placed a bundle on the floor. "Here's the second cot." He glanced at the computer interface. "The password for the computer is Omega Shadows."

"Thanks." Selaynia said to the door as it closed.

* * *

Selaynia had dragged the chair outside of the shelter after reviewing the information on the Kepler-30 system and on Kepler-30d and the moon now called Omega Shadows.

Kepler-30 was one of a number of systems that were discovered in the early twenty-first century, by the Kepler Spacecraft from Earth, as having planetary systems that might be capable of sustaining life. Kepler-30 was a three-planet system with two large gas giants. Omega Shadows was a moon of Kepler-30d, the third planet in the system. Kepler-30d was a hot world and even though Omega Shadows's orbit around the planet partially shielded it from Kepler-30, a mainstream star similar to the Sun of the Sol system, but cooler, the orbit of the planet put it closer to the sun than what was commonly recognized as the habitable zone for a solar system. It was the balance between Omega Shadows's orbital position around Kepler-30d and Kepler-30d's orbital position around its sun that allowed for the formation of a habitable, albeit hot and humid, environment on the moon.

She had watched Kepler-30d where it sat on the horizon of the Omega Shadows. The moon stayed just in the shadow of the planet. Despite being in the shadow of the gas giant, there were still short periods of full daylight and total darkness. Most of the time, however, the moon was in a state of dawn or dusk. Perhaps the reason Nolan had named the place Omega Shadows. She wasn't sure how the orbits were set up to allow that but appreciated the brief hours of cooler temperatures. She had stepped out of the shuttle during the full daylight hours and the temperature had to have been at its peak for the day. Now it had moved from full dark into dawn and the temperature had dropped to a much more reasonable number. After the earlier heat, it even held a chill to it. But with the sun starting to rise, even with the shadow of the gas giant, the day would soon begin warming.

The chill didn't bother her. Her home, Canthralas, had been a cool planet and with the time she had been stuck on

Wyvern, where it didn't get cool, even at night, she welcomed the chill.

The information she had accessed had mentioned only a few life forms on the moon. No big predators and nothing that appeared to be dangerous to humanoid life. There was a small cat-like predator that hunted in the forests. There was mention of several bird-like species and insects. Nothing of any real interest.

:*We need to move away from this area if we are to try and find what we're looking for.*

Selaynia looked down and saw Smokeshadow sitting next to the chair. She was surprised she hadn't heard the wolf push the door open and come out.

:*There are too many other minds here. We will need to find a place where we can block them out and reach out to the one or ones we are seeking.*

"I agree. Any suggestions on which way to go?"

Smokeshadow took a few steps then stopped and appeared to be sniffing the air. :*To the north.*

Selaynia stood and looked in the direction the wolf was facing. Not far from the area was a large hill that rose above the trees.

"Let's see what supplies we can gather up and head out." She opened the door and whistled at the still-sleeping Shadowmist.

"Need a guide?"

Selaynia turned to see McKeon standing a few feet away with two packs in his hands. "Where are you going?"

"We're headed north—to that hill to start."

"We should be there by full dark."

"We?" Selaynia took one of the packs and checked it: Rations, water, a portable shelter and other things that might be needed for a trip.

"Yes, we." McKeon headed toward the hill.

Selaynia tied her long silver hair back into a ponytail and followed McKeon, who had already been joined by Smokeshadow.

:*She thinks McKeon would be a good match for you,* Shadowmist said as he walked beside her.

She ignored the comment.

* * *

McKeon's prediction of making the hill by full dark was on target. Selaynia sat down and motioned for the two wolves to sit next to her. She placed a hand on each of them and opened her mind. She had no idea what she was going to do, but here she could feel the strength of the telepathic field the wolves had been sensing. There was more than one presence in that field. In some ways it reminded her of the wolf song of her home world. Without any other direction, she was going to try the same technique she would use to call a gathering of the packs on Canthralas. She sat on a nearby rock and opened her mind to the field, listening and letting her mind merge with the other presences. She howled as she would have—calling the packs, feeling the song echo through her mind and start changing as it was picked up by the others.

:This is an interesting form.

Selaynia opened her eyes to see a large black wolf standing before her. The wolf's eyes were bright silver and sparkled like the stars in the night sky above them.

"I am—"

:You are called Selaynia and the others are McKeon, Shadowmist and Smokeshadow. We have been studying you and the others since the one you call Nolan crashed here. He was followed by those you call the Rhiash and killed. His consciousness became a part of what we are.

"But, if he is dead..." Selaynia glanced at McKeon who only shrugged.

:His consciousness lives as part of us. And it was his concern for his compatriots that allowed us to send out the shuttles seeking them.

The form of the wolf shifted and it was Nolan standing there. "They call themselves the Bloemetjes, or that is the closest pronunciation. They actually live as part the winds of the planet you call Kepler-30d. But their energy reaches this world as well."

"So you're actually one of these Bloemetjes, not really Conrad Nolan?"

"I am Conrad Nolan and I am also one of the Bloemtjes. His body was destroyed but his consciousness became part of us. But he was trapped here on this world and could not join us in the winds of our home. So we used our strength to bring others here."

"Why the deception when I landed. You acted like you had no idea what this field was. Yet you are a part of it."

"He didn't want to bias you in seeking us out. We knew the one you call Smokeshadow had already sensed us so he figured this was the best way to prevent any potential bias."

Selaynia stood up and held out her hand. "Thank you. But, I need to return to Melpomene. There are people fighting to regain what we lost and I am needed there."

"We understand and you can take the Omega shuttle that brought you here; we have others. Now that we understand more of what has happened to your people we would offer this world as a place where others can come to find a place free from this Confederation. Those that hunt you will not be able to find you.

"There may be others here that will want to return with you. But remember this will be a safe haven for your people— send those who no longer wish or are unable to fight here."

Nolan shifted back to the large black wolf. *:This is an interesting form. It would be interesting to travel with you if you will allow it.*

"Are you still the consciousness of Nolan or one of the Bloemtjes?"

:We are one of the Bloemtjes. Nolan wishes to remain here to guide this colony. He is already explaining what you have learned to the others and letting them decide if they wish to remain or return.

"McKeon? Will you be staying or do you want to go to Melpomene?"

"It seems Smokeshadow thinks I should go with you," he said.

:I told you she thought he was a good match for you. She has bonded with him, Shadowmist said.

Selaynia smiled. It would be an interesting trip back to Melpomene.

Kepler-22

This planet, Kepler-22b, holds a special place in history of the Kepler mission. It was the first small planet discovered by Kepler to reside in the habitable zone of its host star, meaning this planet could potentially harbor life as we know it. At present, we believe it is too large to have a solid surface, probably more like Neptune or Uranus. However, in the mind's eye of this author, such an ice giant planet could have a temperate understory hosting a rather congenial, albeit mixed-up society.

Kepler-22	Stellar Characteristics
Temperature	5518 Kelvins
Mass	0.97 Solar masses
Radius	0.98 Solar radii
Visual Magnitude	12
Distance from Earth	619 Light years

Kepler-22b	Planet Characteristics
Temperature	262 Kelvins
Mass	>36 Earth masses
Radius	2.4 Earth radii
Orbital Period	290 days
Distance from Star	0.85 AUs

Daniel and the Tilmarians
Doug Williams

Daniel sat in the warm light of the small telescope's control room with his grandfather as the first spectra of the night appeared on the computer screen. "I don't see it, Grandpa. Did we pick the wrong planet?" Daniel asked.

"Oh, it's much too early to be disappointed or make assumptions," his grandfather mused. Even my new technique won't be able to distinguish chlorophyll on a planet from the overwhelming light of the parent star with just one image. We'll need to add several images together before we see anything."

"So, we just have to sit here and wait? I thought it was going to be more exciting than this, coming to the observatory and doing astronomy with you." Daniel shuffled his feet and sat on his hands.

"If you want to be the famous and well known scientist you're always talking about, you're going to need more than that new implant and its nanites your parents got you for your birthday. I still think you're too young for such, but that's just my opinion. Anyway, good science takes patience and sometimes long, hard and tedious work."

"I'm not too young for an implant." Daniel's voice raised an octave as he subconsciously reached around and rubbed the skin on the back of his head where the cybernetic implant had been attached to the base of his skull earlier that day. "I'm thirteen. And, that's how old the stupid law says I have to be."

Daniel was impatient with protocols, rules and laws. He considered himself much too intelligent to have to wade through a useless five-year wait until he could legally receive the direct brain implant, along with the adult dosage of nanites. He'd come up with a better plan. For the past several months he had been stealing a few nanites from his parents' dosage caps. Then, just before coming up to the observatory with his grandfather this evening he gave himself an injection, adding to what the technicians had given him earlier. Almost immediately his mind grew more focused. His thoughts and vision became sharp and clear.

"Tell you what," his grandfather said. "Why don't you put that new technology to work and get the weather forecast for this evening. And, if we do discover chlorophyll on one of these Kepler planet follow-up observations, I will put your name on the paper as a collaborator."

"I guess that's acceptable." Daniel looked at the floor, not showing his excitement at the possibility of discovering evidence of life on other worlds. Using the implant, he accessed the cyber net. He felt a surge of satisfaction when the mental action required for the connection was smooth and simple. He hardly felt he'd done anything at all. "It looks like there might be clouds just after midnight, Grandpa. But, we should have some really good observing conditions until then."

"Good. Now help me decide which of these planets we are going to observe next." With that his grandfather pulled up a chart of the Kepler observations that had first been made twenty years earlier.

Just then, Daniel heard an odd sound. It was like a faint whisper, like a light wind through the trees on a nice summer day. Or, did he feel it inside his head? He checked that he had terminated his mental connection with the cyber net. Strange, he didn't recall hearing or reading about anybody reporting such things with new implants. He allowed himself a vague notion that it was a side effect of the extra nanites he'd injected. But, he assured himself he would soon master their behavior.

There it was again, louder! That odd but pleasant sound was definitely inside his head. He could almost understand it, like an emotion rather than a word. It had a sense of concern, almost panic. He glanced up at the guide star monitor. With a start, he said, "Grandpa! The guide star just disappeared."

"What? Why? What's going on?" There was a slight edge of agitation in grandfather's voice mixed with consternation and impatience. "There can't be clouds. It was perfectly clear a half hour ago"

"I don't know," said Daniel. "I just looked at the monitor and saw the star doing its usual little dance around the guide box and it suddenly vanished. It was like something just wiped it away."

"Well, we'd better go out on the catwalk and have a look at the sky. Damnation! I have to finish these observations. This is the last observing run for this project. We can't lose any time."

Even without time for their eyes to adjust to the dark they could tell the sky was clear. The stars shone brightly overhead. The strange sound Daniel heard persisted. It was very clear now, and it conveyed a stronger sense of panic than he'd felt before.

Halfway around the dome's catwalk, on the side facing the big meadow, Daniel saw a weird, faint glow that stood on the far end of the meadow looking like a gigantic walnut. Then he blinked his eyes and it was gone. "Did you see something on the other side of the meadow?"

"I don't see anything." His grandfather brought his gaze down from the sky.

"Probably just the implant playing tricks on me." Daniel gave a half-laugh. He was positive he had seen something, a shimmer like the wavy vision of a mirage on a hot day.

His grandfather's brow furrowed. "You let me know if you see anything else unusual, you understand. Hallucinations are the first sign of problems with an implant—I need to know as soon as possible. Understand?"

"Okay." Daniel was positive it was not a hallucination.

"I'm thinking now, I should have left you at home where you'd be closer to help if things went wrong after your procedure today."

As they reentered the control room, those odd sounds absorbed Daniel's attention. They were calmer now. Strangely, like two thoughts coming together, like a conversation, each time he heard, or felt those sounds his sense of understanding grew.

"...grounded safely on a mountain top ... diagnostics now."

Another disembodied voice answered, "...outside ... scan for damage ... external sensors have also malfunctioned."

"Ah. It looks like our guide star is back." His grandfather indicated the small bright disk centered inside a box displayed on the guiding monitor. "Whatever it was is gone now. We can continue with our observations."

"Yeah, looks like," said Daniel. "Say, Grandpa, I'm going

down to the restroom. Be back after a bit."

"Take your time. We have a few more observations on this target. No rush."

Walking right past the restroom Daniel headed out the ground floor door and around the observatory building. He stopped dead in his tracks as the far end of the meadow came into view.

This was definitely not a hallucination. The shimmer at the far end had become a steady glow. He had seen correctly, it was the shape of a walnut. A very, very large walnut. He also saw two smaller, fainter glowing, shimmering shapes moving on the ground around it.

The almost continuous, weird whispering, swishing was still in his head, but he understood it as a language now. He just didn't know how he was hearing it or why he could understand it. "...the gravity inversion nacelle ring ... no visible damage on this side. Moving to examine all around."

Gradually, he was able to understand more.

"Very good ... alert for indigenous ... We have not completed cataloging the fauna in this area, but we have seen one variety of creature eating our cousin trees on this planet ... gladly eat us as well."

On this planet? Daniel wondered. No. This couldn't be happening. An alien ship landing on the very mountain top where he was. Maybe it is a hallucination. But, Daniel told himself it had to be real.

The voice returned. "The exterior of the conveyance shows no evidence of sabotage."

Daniel's imagination ran full speed. He didn't need any special implant or nanite technology to understand what he was seeing. He considered the direction the telescope pointed when the guide star disappeared, and where this "conveyance" now sat. If it had been flying north to south it could easily have passed in front of the telescope and blocked their view for a moment.

Grandpa will never believe what I'm seeing, Daniel thought to himself. *I really should go get him, but I want to get a closer look first.* Keeping to the shadows, he made his way along the edge of the meadow, but realized he'd come out without a flashlight.

Oddly he didn't really need one. Excited, he concluded the nanites must be enhancing his night vision. *My birthday present is everything I hoped it would be!*

The two shimmering, glowing shapes moved out of view around the side of the big walnut-shaped vessel. Standing at the edge of the meadow, near the ship, Daniel spied an opening in its side he had not seen earlier. He simply could not help himself. He had to go and look.

He stepped onto the bottom of what looked like a ramp extending from the opening. Instantly, he found himself just inside the opening, at the top of the ramp. He marveled at that for a moment while looking back at the observatory dome. Then he turned to face the interior of the ship where the air was much warmer and more humid. He could see only that he was in a small chamber with a warm yellowish glow emanating from the walls, making him feel welcome. No door was visible except for where he'd just come in.

He stepped away from the entrance, exploring. But, he found with each step he became heavier. After four or five steps he could no longer stand. He collapsed on the floor, unable to move. Breathing was difficult. He passed out.

* * *

Daniel awoke feeling groggy and uncomfortably warm, with a noticeable headache. He inhaled only to choke on a breath of hot, heavy, damp air. He found if he inhaled slowly it wasn't quite so bad. In fact he was greeted by a surprisingly pleasant, fresh, floral smell. Disconcerted, he realized the new nanite-borne clarity of thought he experienced was mostly absent. With a slight panic, he mentally cast about for the cyber net. There was no trace of it. His implant could find no connection. The soft, alluring whisper inside his head was barely there. He listened carefully, hearing other strange sounds he was sure were not in his head.

Opening his eyes, he was greeted by that same warm, yellowish light he'd seen inside the entrance to the ship, at the top of the ramp. The walls of the small room where he found himself were covered with beautiful, intricate looking artwork—of plants he guessed—just not any he was familiar with. He moved his arms and legs tentatively, happy not to feel that heavy resistance. As he started to move, the faint whisper in his head coalesced into a voice.

"The creature is stirring. It appears to have regained consciousness."

An opening appeared in one of the warmly glowing, art-covered walls—an opening much wider and taller than any normal door he was used to. Standing there was something that resembled a giant asparagus spear set atop three leg-like stalks. Each of which merged into huge padded feet that reminded Daniel of camel's feet he'd seen at the zoo. Halfway up the smooth, slender, cylindrical trunk, three octopus-like tentacles without the suction cups, sprouted symmetrically around its circumference, each directly above a leg. Each tentacle ended in an array of much smaller tentacles. Above the tentacles, the body was slightly thicker with no obvious neck.

A glittering band wrapped around the body a couple feet above the arms. Daniel grew self-conscious when he realized the wide area of iridescent facets seemed to respond to his every move. Those iridescent facets reminded him of high-res pictures of insect eyes. Only, they weren't eerie like insect eyes. Instead there was a wholesome sense in the way they regarded him. Above that *eye-band* his attention was drawn to the bulbous, spear-shaped top of the creature. It truly looked like the top of a spear of asparagus with its many short stalks ending in pointed, bud-like features all compacted together, forming in a large point a good seven feet above the floor.

Strangely, Daniel did not feel threatened, or at all in danger. In fact, he felt quite safe. And, though he didn't posses the humorous sense of irony that his father seemed to prize, he couldn't help but realize through the dull ache in his head the irony of what stood in front of him.

A voice now sounded inside his head, conveying curiosity. "You find something about us amusing?"

The question shocked Daniel. He hadn't made a sound, hadn't spoken a word. But, the creature even seemed to have inclined its upper body in an almost questioning pose. Giggling, he replied, "You *are* green! Not very little I'd say, but green." His voice sounded loud as he realized the creature in front of him had not spoken. He'd only heard the words in his head.

The creature remained outside the entrance, not moving. "We are not sure we have an accurate translation matrix yet. You find my color amusing?"

"You are an alien, aren't you?" he ventured. "And, I'm on-board your ship, aren't I?"

"I am Astorilangia. Yes, we are from another world. We are explorers."

"How are you talking to me? You don't have a mouth I can see."

"We speak with the mind and with thought."

"Like telepathy? That's a myth. There's no such thing as telepathy."

"Really? Your species doesn't use thought to communicate? We are able to read your thoughts quite easily it seems. We wonder if this is because of the tiny machines we found in your circulatory system. They are intelligent, but they were destructive to your body. When we discovered you unconscious in our air-lock we perceived damage occurring. So, we brought you inside and removed most of them from your body."

"Tiny machines? You mean my nanites? You took my nanites?" Daniel slammed his fists on the platform. "You had no right to do that. How dare you invade my body like that!" But, that did explain the diminished mental clarity.

"I went to a lot of trouble to get those nanites. You've stolen my opportunity to be the greatest, most famous scientist on the planet and to know all there is to know. I want them back, now."

"We felt we had no choice. While the danger wasn't immediate, the damage would have been irreparable, and your brain would have ceased functioning after two to three revolutions of your planet. We did leave a few of them in your body after we discovered, even in your unconscious state, they facilitate our communication with you. It was their large number together that was causing the damage.

"We believed it was because of your tiny machines our conveyance's internal sensors did not actually detect your presence. This we found puzzling until we discovered their quantum signature is very similar to our conveyance's own energy fields. We are sorry, we cannot return them to you. After we removed them from your body we realized they are somewhat superior to similar devices we posses. It became evident we could use them to better repair the sabotage that caused our forced landing on your mountain top. They are now fully integrated with our ship's circuits, and for their use we are grateful."

The creature, Astorilangia—Daniel decided to call it, Astor—stood with its three arms occasionally moving methodically, and its iridescent light receptor array changing hues as its upper torso/trunk turned and twisted slightly. The movement was almost hypnotic. Daniel's anger subsided some when he realized they may have saved his life by removing most of the nanites. But he wasn't willing to concede that he was too young for them. He may have just injected too many, being over enthusiastic about the prospects of their potential.

Though still upset, Daniel was more curious than anything else as he watched the many bud-like stalks of the creature's bulbous, spear-shaped top opening and closing, sometimes all in unison, sometimes one side then the other would open or close, or individual stalks would move on their own. He made as if to swing his legs off the small platform where he found himself. That's when the creature showed how agile and graceful it actually was. With one swift movement, it entered the room and gently blocked Daniel from moving off the platform.

"You must remain on the trundle. Your body is not strong enough to withstand our gravity. The trundle is adjusted to your planet's gravity, and you must remain on it while you are onboard our conveyance."

"And how long will that be? How long has it been? I've got to get back to the telescope. I know my grandfather's getting worked up by now, maybe even worried. I told him I was only going to the restroom."

"You've been with us for half of one of your planet's rotations. We are sure that your presence will be missed, but you cannot go back at this time. We have left your planet's orbit and are in transit back to our world."

"You mean we're not on Earth anymore?"

"No. Our mission was cut short by the sabotage. It is urgent that we return home to resolve this unprecedented act of aggression against our branch of the evolutionary collective. Our mission cannot continue while this threat looms. It would be irresponsible and foolish to do so. This unheard of incident affects our entire society. It is partly why we made the decision to keep you on our conveyance."

"I don't understand."

"Your condition was due to our negligence when we left our entry open. We feel responsible for your becoming trapped by our much higher artificial gravity. We could not just leave you. We are not completely familiar with the indigenous dangers of your planet."

"So, what are you going to do when you get back to your world, declare war on someone?"

The green plant-like being, Astor, stood still, its band of multifaceted eyes changing color and flashing with iridescence even though there was no motion. Its bulbous, pointed top began slowly opening and its individual stalks moved independently, creating the illusion of a light breeze blowing through the branches of a tree. Finally, it answered.

"War. You mean the act of physically attacking another with the intent of bodily harm or destruction?"

"Well, yeah. I guess," Daniel said, carefully. "I mean, that's what it sounded like you had in mind."

"This is not our intent at all. This concept of war was wholly foreign to us before we left our world and began exploring our stellar neighborhood, bringing back stories of other life forms and societies that actually hurt and kill one another.

"No. Such a thing is unlikely with our sister species. We fear that by this act, they are maneuvering for a position of higher leverage within our governing body. It is our contention that by showing us they have the power to harm us, by demonstrating this sort of advantage over us, they wish to force us into some kind of agreement we normally would not accept. What other reason could there be for such outright aggression toward us?"

Daniel shrugged. "My grandpa says that war is a human invention. I don't know if he'd be happy or sad to hear that's not true. But he certainly will be happy to know there is other intelligent life in the universe. In fact, he's an astronomer and I

was working with him to find evidence of other life out there."
Daniel drew a short breath. "And now here you are; the best
proof of all that we're not alone!"

Astor remained motionless.

Daniel sighed. "So, am I a political prisoner that you hope
to use as leverage when you confront—what did you call
them—your sister species?"

"Oh, by no means! No. It was only ensuring your well
being that caused us to leave your planet with you onboard. I
assure you we regret having been forced to act so quickly. You
see, this sabotage made us visible not only to you, but also to
your authorities. Had we not left when we did we likely would
have encountered further problems from the two aircraft that
were coming to intercept us. Yours is a very aggressive society
and it was not our intention to make ourselves known at this
point. We do intend to return you as soon as we have this
problem resolved."

"So what am I supposed to do until then? Sit in this room
on this gravity platform? Can I at least have some food? I'm
starving."

"Yes. Hopefully, this won't be problematic. Come with me,
we will attempt to accommodate your food needs."

Astor extended a tentacle and reached beneath the edge
of the gravity platform. "Your trundle will take you wherever you want. The controls are here." Without turning, Astor
merely moved on its three legs in the other direction as it led
Daniel's *trundle* from the room.

Fascinated, Daniel noted that neither the arms nor the legs
appeared to have joints. They bent or extended smoothly as
it led the way along a wide, but short corridor. When they
reached the end of the corridor the creature mentally articulated the word, "Palumpas", and they were suddenly in a
large, high-ceilinged space filled with plants of all kinds, none
of which Daniel had ever seen before. Thirty-foot tall, tree-
like plants interspersed with flowering shrubbery filled the
space. Dirt, or something that looked like peat moss, actually
covered the floor. It smelled rich and fertile, reminding him
of the arboretum his parents seemed fond of taking him to at
least once a year.

"Welcome to our Palumpas," said Astor. "This is where we take our nourishment and relax. It's the best we can do to replicate our home forest on this small conveyance, but it suffices."

The humidity was more stifling in here but Daniel determined to endure it. Momentarily, he noticed movement nearby. One of the shorter tree-like plants moved its branches. Daniel noticed a slight similarity between it and his host, though it was a good two feet taller. Although it had three arm-like tentacles, like Astor's, it had no legs. Instead, it had a single three-segmented trunk, as though the legs had never separated, and stood on the soil as would any tree. Its overall color was browner than green except for the top spear-like structure which was green, and much fuller, less pointed than Astor's. Nowhere did Daniel see an eye band.

"Ah, this is Peliagantor, a sedentarian—" at least that's what Daniel thought he heard "—of our sister species in the evolutionary collective. They refer to us as activarians because we can move around more readily than they."

Daniel heard a distinctly different voice in his head. It was pleasant and melodious like Astor's, but with a different quality Daniel couldn't identify at first. It said, "The nutrient mixture is synthesized. A receptacle has been extruded."

"Many thanks, Peliagantor." Astor directed Daniel toward the trough. "We have analyzed most of the contents of your digestive system and found that its makeup is compatible with a few substances we have with us. We hope you find it to your satisfaction."

The trough held a thick, tan colored liquid that smelled faintly of fish and chalk. Daniel looked at it with trepidation. "How can I know I won't get sick, or worse, die from eating this ... stuff?"

"We chose your planet to visit because of the single cell plants that grow in your oceans."

"You mean the plankton."

"That is your name for them? Yes, we are interested in cultivating new food sources and we find their chemical structure very efficient and think they would make a rich contribution to our resources. They are quite compatible with our own, and many other chemistries on our planet. Also, in studying many of the other forms of life on your planet we've found most share similar chemical and biological processes with those on our own planet. Although our planet has no creatures like you, or your four legged land dwellers, it does support many creatures that swim in the oceans or fly in the air. This stew is a combination of the swimmers from our oceans and the tiny crawlers and flyers from our forests."

"The fish I can handle, but are you telling me that this slurry is made of insects too?"

Astor made a sound Daniel couldn't interpret, then said, "I will join you in feeding." With that, it lifted one of its massive feet. Daniel stared, open-mouthed as several root-like tentacles extended from recesses in its underside and burrowed into the soil. It settled the foot softly and repeated the process with the other two. All of the little stalks at its top spread apart as each opened wide in response to increased light intensity. "Ah," Astor said. "Nothing like a good mineral, nutrient and light absorption break."

The stew actually turned out to be okay, if not flavorful. Daniel felt better for having eaten, even if he had to scoop it into his mouth with his hand.

* * *

Still somewhat weak from his self-inflicted invasion of nanites, Daniel often had headaches and dizziness, but was recovering. Astor had shown him two other locations on the walnut-ship—as he'd dubbed it—an observation room with a view outside, and a stellar cartography room where their course was charted, but he found he preferred the Palumpas. It was there he met the other two crew members, Makonmidelia and Tormilidpas, tripedal activarians like Astor. He also met the other two sedentarians on the ship, Desimayloni and Riskeatoria. They had been there, unseen on his first visit, seeming to prefer the back area of the Palumpas.

He found the three sedentarians even more fascinating than Astor and the other activarians. They were more playful, less serious. Their game playing was vaguely similar to statistical online games he and his friends liked to play. But, their games were far more sophisticated, being developed to an extraordinarily high level. Playing games was a pastime they appeared passionate about—in an almost neurotic way, he decided.

Daniel loved games of all sorts. He loved mental and intellectual challenges. Among his peers he was quite a formidable game player. But against these adversaries he felt of no challenge. Many of their games he could not even comprehend. The sedentarians repeatedly assured him that, to them, his strategies and style were unfamiliar and unexpected, and therefore of greater challenge than he suspected. He intrigued them and they wanted to learn more about how his thought processes worked.

The sedentarians, Daniel discovered, could actually move around a small amount. Like the activarians, they had extensible roots that they would snake along the ground, dig in, then pull themselves to that spot. They explained to him that was how they grazed their forest, their root tentacles locating prime feeding patches.

* * *

The seemingly endless game playing, however wore out even Daniel. For a diversion, he ventured into the cartography room where he found Tormilidpas. At his request the activarian was showing him their destination. "Here is your planet," said Tormilidpas, extending one of its many tentacle-like fingers to point at a 3-D image of their local part of the Milky Way, the display perspective adjusted as though seen from near Earth. Then, it pointed to a tiny, faint star saying, "And here is our planet, Tilmaria."

Thrilled, Daniel said, "Hey, that's the Kepler field. See, there's Vega and Deneb. I recognize it from an image my grandfather had. You're from Kepler-22b? That was going to be my choice for the next planet to look at with the telescope."

Tormilidpas then proceeded to show him other planets with life they had visited, some with intelligent life, some without. "We have traveled many places but have yet to find an intelligent species similar to our own." Its voice actually sounded sad.

"You know," Daniel responded tentatively, "that brings up a question I had."

Tormilidpas merely stood there.

"Well, I've been spending a lot of time in your Palumpas, with the sedentarians."

"This we know."

"I was wondering. They tell me they've been confined there, prevented from interacting with the ship's systems and not allowed to leave, when normally they're a part of the crew and free to move anywhere around the ship, on trundles like mine. I'm just curious. Why are they confined there, like prisoners?"

Tormilidpas merely stood there, his top-stalks flexing, more than casually. His ever-changing iridescent eye band suddenly shifted colors more rapidly. Then he replied, "Yes, we have decided you may have this information. It is this sedentarian monad we suspect of being responsible for the sabotage which ultimately brought you among us. Their absence from the normal operation of this conveyance does make the task more difficult for us. They have skills we simply do not posses. But, we find it prudent and necessary to severely limit their normal duties, and access among our conveyance's systems."

"What exactly are their duties?" Daniel had no idea, really, what was required to operate a space ship, let alone an alien space ship. "I mean, all they seem to do is play games."

Again, Tormilidpas stood with stalks flexing and eye band shifting color. For a moment Daniel worried he was being a pest. But, so far he'd been amazed with how both the activarians and sedentarians were very straight forward with him, and how cordial, and friendly they seemed. When he thought about it, he'd never really considered how aliens might act but, somehow, in his mind he'd expected them to be ugly and mean. These aliens, these Tilmarians, were completely the opposite.

"Yes, their game," said Tormilidpas. "That is who they are. It is how they solve mathematical or technical and other tough problems for us. It is how they analyze the world about us. We don't do well thinking in a technical, or an analytical manner ourselves. That is how they function. It is their forte and our weakness. They love games but we really don't have time for them."

"You don't play any games with them?" Daniel asked.

"We understand that is how they interface with each other,

with us and the rest of the world. In a sense, it is their language and so, yes, we play along with their game in as far as we need to communicate and interact with them. We do not pass our time playing their game. We love art and philosophy and dreaming great dreams. These things matter very little to them. In fact, we are not sure they can even comprehend art or dreams any more than we can understand the true nature of their game playing. It is sensible to acknowledge their game playing as their art, though they would say it is their reality.

"Our two species cannot live apart. They tell us how to build the things we conceive of, and we keep their feeding patches fertile and replete with nutrients and minerals. Since they have no physical sight, like us, we allow them to live vicariously through our telepathic sharing. This is how our two species have evolved from the mere shrubbery we were of aeons ago.

"On this conveyance they perform the intricate, often instantaneous calculations needed to manipulate our ship's mass and navigate gravity wells, or to plot our course through, and enter into folded space. Their absence would make our voyage impossible."

* * *

In the Palumpas, Daniel asked the ship for some food as he'd been taught by Astor. A trough, containing his never-changing stew mixture, extruded from the wall. While scooping it to his mouth by hand he was surreptitiously greeted by the sedentarians and asked to join them in a new game.

"Your presence, as an alien, presents us with a unique opportunity to explore in greater depth, our present game, and possibly uncover the true intent behind the progressing stratagem of the activarians. They appear close to winning this current round."

Daniel felt suddenly apprehensive. Though, unable to articulate exactly why, he agreed to join in. Regardless, as the game ensued he marveled, as he had all along, at a fascinating telepathic skill the sedentarians employed. In this game, as with others he'd played with them, they easily shared something he came to think of as the *mental screen*. It was more than a virtual image within which many of their games were played.

It existed directly in his mind.

"Who devises these scenes, these settings where your games are set?" Daniel asked them. "Some of them are strange, kind of dream-like, or like a bizarre fantasy world. Others, like this one are set in a forest that's kind of like here, in your Palumpas."

After a moment of puzzled discussion amongst themselves the sedentarians answered. "Our, settings, as you refer to them, are how we perceive the world. But, the current depiction is one of many shared with us by the activarians. We think their imagination is grand, and are envious of how they conceive of such fantastic and unbelievable mental images."

"But, that's what they see…" he started to say, then thought better of it and chose to continue in the game instead.

They cast him in the role of an activarian. But, oddly they didn't allow him any leeway to improvise, as in other games. He felt like a puppet being told what to do and precisely what to say. As the game progressed, it became obvious it was a reenactment of the so-called mission that his hosts, the Tilmarians, were currently on.

He was surprised at the next line they supplied him with. Suspicious, he went ahead, as an activarian, mentally articulating it anyway. He wanted to see what would follow.

"For this next mission we would ask your help with anything you can do to make this exploration more challenging than what we normally face."

And so, he watched as they created a virus that would infect the guidance and gravity manipulation systems of the ship, along with a few other systems such as external sensors.

Incredulous, he stepped out of character. "Are you saying the activarians wanted you to sabotage this ship and your mission?"

All three sedentarians stopped in dead silence, as if he had breached some sacred game protocol. Within the mental playing screen all three were intently focused on Daniel. He could feel the private communication transpiring between them, though he knew not what was being said. Momentarily they addressed him in voices of accusation, as though they'd been betrayed.

"We've had our suspicions," they said, "but now we are certain. We know now that we are not on a conveyance, as you would have us believe, in this fictitious *outer space*. You are a very clever activarian whom we've never met before, and you hide your true nature from us very well, making us perceive you as an alien being. There are no other beings in the world. All of these other worlds and this, outer space you introduced into our game ages ago do not exist. You hold onto it so stubbornly, as though you're trying to convince us of something we do not, and cannot perceive exists. It is some kind of ploy to deceive us. To what end we have not deciphered yet. But, you are manipulating us for some reason, that part is clear to us now.

"This is a strange and unprecedented tactic you've thrown into the game. Why do you lie to us now and suggest that you asked of us something different than what actually transpired? There is only our world and in proving this, we will win this longest of all games ever played."

Realizing he'd stumbled onto something strange and very real to these beings, Daniel remained quiet. He remembered reading about people, even today, who believe that the Earth is flat. Even when confronted with all the evidence showing that it is indeed a sphere they staunchly, even viciously continue their denial, and refuse to believe anything other than that the Earth is flat.

To the sedentarians, he realized this game, all games, were their real existence. It seemed almost psychopathic but it was their reality. He suddenly became afraid, and in his best gaming manner he ended this session.

After that, Daniel avoided the Palumpas except when he was hungry. When he did go there, he carefully avoided the sedentarians and their pretentiously apologetic requests that he continue the game with them. Instead, he passed his time in the *star lounge,* watching the stretched out starlight passing in their rainbow of colors. There he saw all three activarians on a regular basis as their duty shift revolved.

He liked talking to Tormilidpas the best, and learned that exploration of space was very much an art form for them. The way Tormilidpas talked of their travels made it sound like a dance they were perfecting. Its voice always sounded like a symphony in Daniel's head. It was then he realized the word he'd been searching for since he'd first heard the difference between the two species' mental voices. Timbre. That was it! That was the difference.

While the mental voices of both species sounded sweet and melodious, and combined intricate harmonies, the sedentarians lacked a certain quality of the activarians' voices. The sedentarians' voices had a clear, clean, crisp quality that was very precise. But, the activarians' voices had a quality of sound richer than any music he'd ever heard—both soothing and inspiring. The voices of the sedentarians, pleasant as they were, just seemed utilitarian in comparison. Their voices lacked timbre.

His history of music class last year had talked about just this sort of thing in the evolution of recording media. The old phonograph records, like the ones at his grandfather's house. The ones he only ever regarded as old fogy curiosities, plagued with background noise as they were, really did have a richer sound than the background-quieted digital recording methods now used.

The Tilmarians—activarians and sedentarians—are themselves a duality, he realized. The two species have two complementary perceptions and ways of thinking. The activarians are the analog aspect of the species and the sedentarians the digital. The sedentarians have all the abilities a neuroscientist might attribute to the left side of the human brain while the activarians have attributes more related to the right side of the brain. The activarians have evolved eyes and tripedal locomotion while the sedentarians lead a discrete, mostly stationary existence. Like a quantum of light, with its dual particle and wave aspects, the Tilmarians had taken two distinct, but intertwined evolutionary paths. Now, they were both sides of the same coin. How strange, he thought to himself when he pondered the miscommunication between the two, that often times there is loss of information when an analog signal is transformed into a digital one.

He realized at the same time an even more important truth. This is how he would make a name for himself. It seemed like his destiny, now. He felt certain he would be known as the first human in history to make contact with an alien species, live among them and travel to their planet and he would help them solve a major social crisis. This would be his contribution to his grandfather's work.

* * *

"Our friend, Daniel, that is a truly groundbreaking and revolutionary conclusion. One we might never have come to on our own." Astor stood as though taking in the scene of passing starlight. Daniel couldn't really tell. To him the Tilmarian had no front or back. It faced all directions at once. Its top stalks moved almost frenetically. "We agree we are lucky to have found you among us. An observer from the outside can sometimes see so much more than we can."

"Like seeing the forest for the trees?" Daniel ventured to ask.

Stalks flexing some more, Astor stood a moment. "This we are unable to interpret. Nonetheless, our transit to Tilmaria comes to an end soon. We must make preparations."

Daniel definitely sensed titillation in Astor as it moved to the transport spot and disappeared from the *star lounge*.

He remained and watched the rainbow streaks of light shorten and resolve into points of light as they left hyper-light speed. Soon a large sphere of swirling clouds swung in to fill the view. He estimated he'd been with the Tilmarians, in their walnut-ship, about ten days, and now he would soon be landing on their planet, Tilmaria.

They eventually cleared the bottom of the clouds and what Daniel saw below was beautiful, a land that was pure emerald green in all directions. After flying along at a steady altitude for quite some time they approached the edge of the land where a turquoise ocean filled the horizon. Their horizontal motion ceased and they began a slow vertical decent.

They descended into a forest of absolutely huge trees. Some looked to be a thousand feet tall. They landed in a large clearing where four other similar looking walnut-shaped ships lay at rest.

Outside the ship, many hundreds of plant people of both species had gathered in the clearing as Astor led Daniel on his trundle and the crew, including the three sedentarians each on their own trundle, away from the ship. They went right to the top of a small rise in the center of the clearing.

Astor stood on top the rise for quite some time, waiting as Tilmarians of both species, either walking on three legs or riding on anti-gravity trundles filled the clearing completely. Many of them arrived from the forest canopy above, descending to the ground. Many hundreds more of the plant people perched high above on the huge lower branches of the trees. After a considerable delay, Astor addressed the gathering. Its telepathic voice inside Daniel's mind still had the pleasant resonance he'd become used to, but held an additional aberrant quality.

"Family," Astor began, "much has transpired for us on this latest venture. New and unprecedented experiences have chanced upon us. Not the least of which was our unplanned encounter with a member of an intelligent alien species. It is this one who may have changed the course of our entire society merely by being an outside observer. We owe it, Daniel, our deepest gratitude and will endeavor to respect the revelation its insight has given us by exploring to their fullest, all the possibilities its observation has suggested. We can only seek to strengthen our interspecies sisterhood with this deeper understanding of ourselves."

Though Astor continued on at great length Daniel ceased to hear much of it. He was beside himself with happiness as he gazed around the giant forest clearing. He had achieved something great.

* * *

Greatness was what he fully expected to be known for as the walnut-ship entered Earth's atmosphere a month later. But, to his great dismay the ship didn't go to Washington D.C. like he'd told them they needed to. He had told Astor that they must introduce themselves to the president and make themselves known to all of Earth, and tell everyone what he had done for them.

No, he easily recognized his home town and the nearby mountains as the walnut-ship flew, in the early evening twilight, toward the very spot where they had picked him up. The ship landed at the end of the meadow, near the observatory dome. After a short round of goodbyes, he was told that they had no intention of making themselves known to his world just yet. Daniel stepped off the trundle at the entry where he'd first become trapped and instantly found himself at the base of the ramp. He turned to look back, but the opening had been sealed.

In a great state of consternation and disappointment, he moved off to sit on a rock at the edge of the meadow. Nobody would ever believe him. How could he ever convince anyone that he'd just been on a great adventure? He looked toward the walnut-ship, but it was unseen. He felt, more than heard it repel itself from Earth's gravity and leave. Daniel just sat, looking at the dome as the shutter began to open for the night. The pleasant swish and whisper of the Tilmarians mental voices faded from his mind.

Kepler-35

Kepler-35 is a binary star system containing two nearly identical stars in a tight orbit. The two stars are each slightly smaller and cooler than our sun. A large gas giant planet, a planet slightly smaller than Jupiter, orbits the pair. As we know in our solar system, large planets have fairly large moons and usually more than one. Here is a story of nosy cops, judgmental tourists, and a love that transcends space as well as our typical expectations.

Kepler-35 A,B	Stellar Characteristics
Temperature	5606 / 5202 Kelvins
Mass	0.89 / 0.81 Solar masses
Radius	1.03 / 0.79 Solar radii
Visual magnitude	15.7
Distance from Earth	5363 Light years
Orbital Period	20.7 days

Kepler-35b	Planet Characteristics
Temperature	420 Kelvins
Mass	40.4 Earth masses
Radius	8.2 Earth radii
Orbital Period	131.5 days
Distance from Star	0.4 AU

Exposure at 35b
Mike Wilson

The binary system that grew larger in his view screen never failed to impress Lance. A larger sun circled with a smaller, and a lone gas giant orbited both. Gorgeous celestial scenery seemed appropriate for another rendezvous with the focus of his affections. But Kepler-35 was a fairly popular tourist destination. He would have to keep well clear of the orbiting planet where the viewing colony was situated, if he wanted any privacy. Not that it made any difference.

They could not, would not stop him from seeing and being with his love. Lance already felt her gentle telepathic caress from a thousand kilometers distant. He leaned his lanky body forward, and squinted out his viewing glass, then said, "magnify 5X." Scratching his mop of red hair, he scanned his console indicators. The rental craft was operating about as well as could be expected. With luck, it should get him back by the finish of his two-day.

The center of his view-screen enlarged, and showed her distant figure. She was roughly circular, covered with jutted peaks and dimples. He loved every pinprick and valley of her being.

#My lovely human, you are finally back,# she sent into his mind. He formed clear word-thoughts back, just as she had helped him learn, that first time they met last year.

#It was too long being away from you, darling. I was delayed by local police again.#

#Why do your people give us so much trouble, Lance-human?#

#They do not comprehend our togetherness. They think it is wrong, unnatural,# Lance sent back.

She was filling the center of his view screen now, so he ordered "Normal viewing 1X" out loud. His compact space flitter was slowing, emitting last-minute maneuvering bursts. Lance tolerated the jerky ride; if the rental company knew how he was using it, they would probably not have leased it to him. His two-day leave was just beginning, and he had already used up three hours to get to their rendezvous point here at Kepler-35. As he got closer, more of her detail emerged. He marveled at her complexity. Her outward appearance was that of a rounded asteroid, covered with protrusions and yellow and pink depressions. A bright intelligence burned within! She was one of the Thistles, a very ancient race that humankind had discovered in the last century. The encounters were difficult and deadly at first, but gradually the two races reached accommodation, and even at times, friendship.

They had taught humankind to communicate telepathically with them. Thistles' natural ability had created all kinds of complications. Until recently, these had never involved affairs of the heart.

Lance programmed the flitter to circle at scan range, approximately 50 meters. And then Lance soon forgot the flitter or any kind of outward reality. She took him in a telepathic embrace, with his full acquiescence.

Held in a state of affectionate euphoria, his ecstatic thrills fed back into her larger mind, and set off mini-earthquakes all over her surface. The feedback from that caused him to shake and shudder with sheer loving delight in his light synth jumpsuit. He knew this was going to happen, and was happily prepared to take the brunt of her loving. She relented, and they both went into a calmer state of communion.

They sent back and forth messages of love, interspersed with news and small talk. Finally, Lance simply sank into a light sleep, grabbing a needed rest so his body could replenish itself a little. Sensing his need for down-time, La'Teisha withdrew her thoughts, and let her beloved sleep. They still had another Earth day before he had to return.

Lance soon became aware that something was amiss. He usually awoke after an hour or so, took some refreshment, and they continued their whirling mental dances and interactions. This time he was awoken by three Galactic Patrol ships that came in from a high vector, and surrounded them, their surfaces aglow with red and blue coruscations.

"Unauthorized Flitter, this is GalPatrol. Repeat, this is GalPatrol. Acknowledge immediately or you will be seized and boarded!"

Lance came to, and groggily tried to get his bearings.

'Wha ... where am I? Oh, yeah. Me and La'Teisha were—oh yes.' He heard the commands repeated, blaring out of the flitter's emergency audio.

"Okay, okay. This is Operator Third Class Lance Behrens. I have manifests ready for scanning. What do you want?"

"Operator Lance, are you aware that your ship is in synchronous orbit with a corpus that is forbidden?"

"Oh, the Thistle? This Thistle is my friend. Surely this sector has not outlawed friendship?"

The speaker was silent for several moments.

"You and this Thistle are at an unsafe distance. You are both drifting towards Kepler-35b and Colony Castelia. We merely wish to warn and assist. Do you require assistance?"

Lance wanted to guffaw. He had to be a million klicks distant from Colony Castelia—on purpose, too. Once he had given the legally required ACK and offered his manifests for inspection, there was not a thing they could do, and they knew it. No laws were being broken here, except those of propriety in some humans' eyes.

"No, guys. I'm nominal here. Actually, I am really fine. Your proximity warning is noted, and I thank you for your assistance."

Another silence.

"Very well, Flitter Capricorn and O3C Behrens. Your position is being relayed for safety and order. Thank you and show care."

"Acknowledged, GalPatrol Officers. Show care."

Lance barely suppressed a gag as he exchanged the last pleasantries. But better to be kind than invite trouble. They would probably broadcast the position of the human and his Thistle lover soon.

#La'Teisha love. I fear we may have to cut this short.#

A wave of compassion and affection enfolded him, almost making him cry out. She had suppressed her abilities—good thing, that would have really caused trouble. Now she was letting it all come out. Lance felt like he was ready to burst when she sent that level of emotion his way.

#Scale it back, hon.#

#All right—just got carried away.# The overwhelming

sensations ebbed, and Lance felt like he could breathe again.

#Now, where were we before we were interrupted?#

"#You were resting. But let's enjoy a brief time, and then we should depart.#"

Before Lance could even answer, he felt erotic tendrils of sensation coming off of her surface making his skin practically glow with sensation. His body soon shook with waves of pleasure, making him gasp with delight. The sensation made him blind and disconnected from all of his senses; he felt as though he were at the center of one of the binary suns, glowing and burning hotter than they were. It was not unpleasant, but rather all-encompassing. Lance felt like he was in heaven. She flooded him thus for a time, and then let him be.

#There—that ought to hold you.#

When Lance recovered enough to answer, he sent back, *#Thank you, from the bottom of my soul. You are truly one of a kind.#*

Darker feelings emanated. Lance hastily backpedalled.

#I only meant that as a compliment. You know how much I love you.#

#I know you love what I give you. But do not concern yourself, Human-Lance. I cannot blame you for what others of your race do.#

Mixed feeling surfaced in Lance. But they were interrupted by voices on his comm. They had more company. Spectators. Idiots.

"Hey, look at the freak show!"

"Hey you pervert, leave that Thistle alone!"

"They're both creeps!"

Darn tourists from Castelia must have found us.

Lance finally got the volume turned down.

#La'Teshia, we have visitors. Our position is known. I should go.#

Dark emanations erupted. *#I can get rid of them.#*

Lance felt real fear. If she sent the brats into a panic, they might fire on him or her. He endured a few waves of her blasts of anger, mixed with terrors, and then intervened.

#Okay La'Teisha, please tone it down now.#

The radio chitchat went silent. There were a few curses, and then loud static. The goons were exiting under full power.

Probably teenagers out for a lark. They had gotten more than they bargained for.

#How was that, Human-Lance?#   La'Teisha was enjoying herself.

#That was great, La'Teisha. But now we really need to get going. We are compounding our problems more the longer we stay here.#

#Very well, Lance. Until next two-day then.   You have my love.#   And then she closed herself off from all further communication, and began outgassing puffs from her mottled surface. Lance realized she was unhappy about the parting, but felt there was nothing he could do. He looked at his console, and began to plot his return to the world he resided on, almost a light year distant.

She was miffed. But I can't help the prejudice that exists.   When even teenagers can find out where two dissimilar races are hooking up, and harass them, he thought to himself.

Lance tried to compose his nearly exhausted body, and focus on getting himself home. When he finally had his course plotted and laid in, he executed a burn command, and his hyper-fusion engine lit for just the right duration. He let the acceleration force him back, trying to relax. When the burn finished, he shakily got out some nutri-bars and water, and took refreshment.   He then relieved himself, and finally laid back and dropped off into a heavy sleep.

His dreams were populated with bursts of pleasure, punctuated by dark tendrils of fear and foreboding. As much as he wanted to keep this love affair going, he knew it was going to be fraught with difficulty. But somehow he also knew deep down that he would not be dissuaded, by law enforcers, hecklers or even disapproving family members. Kepler-35 faded to a flickering binary image on a console display, as his spacecraft took him back home. His affections, and concerns, would not fade so easily.

Kepler-17

Ahoy maties … Avast and stand ready. This be a terrible alien solar system for ye exploring. Thy sun-like star makes thee planet Kepler-17b hot as Hades. Ye also ner can stand thy dangers of the deep magnetic potential thy be encountering. Tis not a place for the faint of heart. But for Cap'n Firebrandt, tis jus another harbor in the storm. Shiver me deck plates and pass the rum. Arrrrrrrrrrrrrrrrr

Kepler-17	Stellar Characteristics
Temperature	5630 Kelvins
Mass	1.1 Solar masses
Radius	1.0 Solar radii
Visual magnitude	14
Distance from Earth	1298 Light years

Kepler-17b	Planet Characteristics
Temperature	1570 Kelvins
Mass	779 Earth masses
Radius	14.7 Earth radii
Orbital Period	1.5 days
Distance from Star	0.03 AUs

Hot Pursuit
David Lee Summers

Carter Roberts, first mate of the privateer vessel *Legacy*, entered the bar of Space Station Xiūxí qū sān. The dank hole of dark metal held only two tables and smelled of vomit and cheap booze. The bartender wore a stained, white apron and leaned on the dented counter, eyes half closed. A video screen above the bar displayed the names of drinks along with images of people enjoying them on some faraway resort planet.

Roberts stepped up to the counter. "Rum."

The bartender dropped a plastic cup on the counter and filled it half full from an unmarked bottle. The first mate suspected the same bottle was used no matter what was ordered. The bartender swung a greasy payment pad around, and Roberts swiped a card loaded with credits carefully routed from several bank accounts, none of which actually belonged to him.

He grabbed his cup and moved toward the table furthest from the door. One of the seats was covered in something slimy and unidentifiable. Roberts opted to sit at the other table. He lifted the plastic cup and the contents smelled like rocket fuel. He ventured a taste anyway, and was even more suspicious that the bartender only sold one type of booze—and that it might be equally good at cleaning out toilets as intoxicating the drinker.

A man in a suspiciously good suit stepped into the bar. He evaluated the counter and the unshaven man behind it, then turned to Roberts without ordering anything. "Are you Mr. Wong?" he asked.

"Depends on who's asking?" Roberts took a sip of the "rum" and tried not to grimace.

The man sat down and retrieved a cigarette from a case. He offered one to Roberts, who declined. He decided the cheap booze would make him ill enough without adding the buzz from whatever weed the man was smoking.

"I'm Mr. Wright." The man turned his head and lit the cigarette. "I'm told Mr. Wong has an heirloom for me."

"More of a legacy, actually."

Mr. Wright scowled. Roberts knew he was being a little too overt, but he didn't care. They would be long gone before anyone figured out he'd spoken the name of his ship and that Mr. Wright was arranging transportation.

Roberts sat back and folded his arms. "If you're ready, we could go take a look and see if it's satisfactory."

"I'm sure it will be. We need to retrieve my … charge on the way. Do you want to finish your drink?"

"I'd rather not." Roberts stood.

The man who called himself Wright dropped the cigarette to the deck and crushed it under his shoe, then led the way out of the bar through a series of pipe-lined tunnels to a bank of storage lockers. He dug through his pockets for a key, opened one of the lockers and retrieved a large duffel bag. Presumably it contained the item he was responsible for—his charge.

With the first mate in the lead, they wound their way back through the maze of corridors. As they turned the corner into the station's reception area, they were greeted by four men and two women in gray uniforms without insignia. A blond haired man stepped forward. "We need to see your passports."

Roberts shook his head. "You don't look like station personnel to me. Your uniforms are much too new." He wondered how strangers to the station could know how to find them so quickly. Perhaps he really should have been more careful speaking at the bar.

"Can we see some identification?" asked Mr. Wright smoothly.

The uniformed agents drew heplers—high-energy pulse guns. "I believe you're carrying contraband in your luggage, sir. We need to inspect it."

"You don't look like customs officials, either," said Roberts. "I suggest you let us pass."

"We're the ones with the guns," said the blond man.

High-energy pulses tore through the uniformed man and woman who stood at each end of the line blocking Roberts and Wright. The first mate smiled as he saw Captain Firebrandt of the *Legacy* behind the uniformed strangers. Nicole Lowry stood next to him, hepler at the ready. Alarm klaxons sounded as sensors detected the weapons' fire. Station police would be there soon.

The four remaining agents crouched low and formed a circle. Wright drew a pistol from inside his jacket as Roberts ducked back into the corridor for cover. The blond man fired, burning a hole through Wright's chest. Roberts grimaced. They could still salvage the cargo, but without the courier, they had no idea what it was or where to deliver it. That made collecting payment difficult.

Lowry and Firebrandt took out two more of the agents. Roberts pulled his own hepler and took aim from his position of cover. He fired at the blond man who dove out of the way.

The remaining woman stood, holding up her hands. The blond agent let out a cry of rage and aimed at her. As he did so, both Firebrandt and Lowry fired at him. One pulse went through his chest, the other through his head.

Roberts heard footsteps from behind. He rushed into the reception area and grabbed Wright's duffel bag. He almost toppled over as he tried to lift it. It was much heavier than it looked. He hefted it and tottered toward the airlock. Seeing his difficulty, Lowry ran out and gave him a hand.

Just then, station police appeared in the corridor. Firebrandt lay down covering fire as Roberts and Lowry carried the load past him. Once they entered the ship, Firebrandt darted back through the airlock, closed the door, and rushed forward, along the corridor. Roberts and Lowry left the parcel against the wall and followed on his heels.

"Detach from the station and find me the nearest jump point away from here," said Firebrandt as he reached the battle deck.

"Aye, aye, sir," said Kheir el-Din. The helmsman stood at a console at the center of the deck. His long beard was twisted into several thin braids with beads at the ends.

"Scanning jump point catalog," said Computer, a pale, thin man who had a neural net strung through his brain, which gave him instant access to all functions of the ship's computer and much of the galactic network.

Roberts proceeded forward to his station near the holographic tank that filled the battle deck's bow. He activated his console and monitored both Computer's search and el-Din's maneuvers.

The *Legacy* gracefully rolled away from the space station as a series of tiny spheres materialized in the holographic tank showing the positions of jump points. One of them began flashing green.

"Nearest jump point leads to Kepler-17, an active G2 star with no inhabited planets," reported Computer faster than Roberts could scan the search results.

"Make for that," ordered the captain. "Hopefully it'll give us time to figure out what that courier had and what to do with it."

As the captain spoke, a course projection appeared in the holographic tank and a warning light flashed on Roberts's console. "Two ships have just disengaged from the station. I'm guessing they have an interest in Mr. Wright's package," said the first mate.

"Stay on course to the jump point," said the captain.

"They'll just follow us through," protested the helmsman.

Firebrandt nodded. "Sure, but if we get there ahead of them, we might find someplace to hide before they get there, or maybe another jump point." He retrieved a pipe and a pouch of tobacco from his pocket. "Computer, what can you tell me about Kepler-17?"

The view in the holographic tank dissolved into a schematic of the star system. A planet orbited so close to the star, it nearly touched the surface. "Kepler-17 is an extremely active star with an intense magnetic field."

Firebrandt folded his arms and considered the schematic. After a moment, he pointed to the hologram. "What can you tell me about the planet close to the star?"

"It's a Jovian planet known as Kepler-17b with a period of approximately 1.5 days."

Nicole Lowry let out a long, low whistle. "Sounds a bit torrid for my taste."

Roberts scowled as he checked his monitor. "Those ships that disengaged from the station are definitely on an intercept course. They've nearly matched our speed and they're accelerating."

Firebrandt's brow furrowed as he packed tobacco into the pipe. "Who are these people?" He tucked the tobacco pouch back in his coat pocket. "Will they catch us before we make it through the jump point?"

Roberts ran a calculation, then shook his head. "Not unless they're magicians who can exceed the speed of light in normal space."

The captain placed the pipe in his mouth and lit it as he considered the schematic. "Once we jump, can we make it to that planet near the star before those cruisers catch us?"

The first mate considered the numbers on his screens. "Depends a bit on who they are and whether they want to capture whatever's in that bag. They'd have a hard time disabling us before we got in near the planet, but if they don't care about being subtle, they could throw enough heavy fire our direction to blow us out of the sky."

Firebrandt looked up at the chronometer and Roberts followed his gaze. They were nearly at the jump point. "After we come out of jump, take Lowry and look in that duffel. I want to know our options. Should we just give it to them and cut our losses, or is it something valuable we want to hang on to?"

"Aye, aye, sir," said Roberts as Lowry nodded.

"We're at the jump point for Kepler-17," reported Computer.

"Head for that planet—17b—as soon as we're on the other side. Best speed."

* * *

Suki Mori's eyes flew open and her tablet fell to the deck with a thud. She had fallen asleep while reading and dreamed she was back on the planet Prospero. In the dream, the door to her apartment exploded inward. Six men in gray uniforms with no insignia charged in and grabbed her. She knew at once they were soldiers of fortune, employed by a crime boss named Chris Bowman.

Breathing heavily she looked around the cabin, reminding herself that she was safe—at least mostly. She had been rescued by Captain Firebrandt and was now aboard the *Legacy*. Soon after her rescue, she had discovered that Firebrandt was a pirate. One criminal had rescued her from another. She hijacked the *Legacy* so she could return to her parents who worked as mineralogists in the asteroid belt of Earth's solar system. The pirates foiled her attempt and the captain nearly ordered her executed. She was spared when she rescued the pirate crew from an enemy warship.

Now she was in a state of limbo. Over time, she had earned the freedom to move about the ship and the captain was warming up to her again, but she had no desire to be part of a pirate crew. At the same time, she didn't dare anger Firebrandt again. So, she did her best to perform jobs the crew requested and stay out of the way the rest of the time.

When she heard the *Legacy* was picking up a mysterious package and courier at Space Station Xiūxí qū sān, she figured she should remain in her cabin until they were underway. She picked up the fallen tablet and checked the computer display. The ship had just disengaged from the station's airlock. That's probably what jarred her awake.

The engines ramped up and a quick check of the ship's computer confirmed they were in motion. A few minutes later, she heard the jump warning. She secured her tablet and strapped herself in. After a moment, all sense of direction was lost as the ship leapt beyond normal three-dimensional space into a realm where left, right, up, down and the march of time held no meaning—or more precisely, they were no longer the limits of meaning.

A short time later, reality snapped back into focus. The jump was complete. Suki figured it was safe to find out what was going on. She unbuckled her harness and left the cabin. Walking along the corridor, she noticed a duffel bag abandoned against the wall.

Curious, she opened it up. Inside was a metallic device that looked like three spheres welded end-to-end. She rolled it over and saw several sockets that looked like power feeds and data connections. Rolling it a little further, she found an input screen. She pushed a black button next to the screen and a menu appeared. "Huh…" she said as she considered the options presented to her.

"Back away from that … slowly."

She looked up and saw Roberts and Lowry. Roberts drew a hepler pistol and aimed it at her. She held her hands aloft, stood, and took a careful step backward.

"What are you doing, Ms. Suki?" asked Lowry.

"Sorry, I just saw this in the corridor and was trying to fig-ure out where it belonged."

"Where it belonged," said Roberts, "or what it does?"

Suki's eyebrows came together. "What it does might tell me where it belongs..." She shook her head.

"We were ambushed," said Lowry, softly. "We're being pursued."

Roberts nodded and took a step toward Suki. "You've wanted off this ship. Did you find someone to help you?"

Suki shook her head and frowned. "All the captain told me was that you were picking up a courier of some kind. If I was going to try to leave the ship, the last place I'd do it is a back-water hole like Xiūxí qū sān."

Roberts nodded. She didn't think he was thoroughly satis-fied, but he seemed impatient with something more than her. "So, did you learn anything?" he asked.

Suki let out a breath she didn't know she was holding. "Is this thing even real? According to the diagnostic screens, this generates nodal points to go beyond space." She shook her head. "Could it be a gravity wave sensor like those they use on mapping vessels?"

Roberts handed Lowry the hepler, knelt down by the de-vice and began scrolling through the menus. His brow fur-rowed. "My God, I think you may be right about this. It does look like some kind of nodal point generator." He looked up. "We better inform the captain." He stood and grabbed Suki by the arm, turning her toward the battle deck. Although she sensed the first mate's anger, she didn't feel danger as she had from Bowman's men back on Prospero.

"What do you mean by a 'nodal point generator'?" asked Lowry as they marched down the corridor.

Suki shrugged free from Roberts's grip. "How well do you understand jumps?"

"You can imagine space as a surface like a piece of paper and we're a flat object confined to the surface that can't per-ceive up or down." Lowry held her hand palm-up and traced a path with the index finger of her other hand. Then she cupped her hand. "However, gravity bends space. We can use that fact to jump the gap, moving quickly from one point to another." She moved her finger in the cupped hollow of her palm.

"That's basically it," said Suki. "Jump points are those places where we can easily go beyond the three physical dimensions we know." She looked over her shoulder. "I think that device can be used to generate a jump point anywhere, not just a place where gravitational fields converge."

Lowry's eyebrows came together. "You've gotta be kidding me."

"Such a thing would be worth a fortune," said Roberts as they entered the *Legacy's* battle deck. "Well worth the danger of betraying us."

Suki scowled. "I would have needed to know about it to make a deal to sell it." She snorted, then her eyes widened as she saw the view in the holographic tank.

They were approaching a turbulent, yellow star with numerous spots darkening its surface. A prominence formed a hellish arch thousands of kilometers above the star's surface. Beyond that and impossibly close to the star was a banded planet, like Jupiter—although if she believed the numbers floating in the holographic tank, the planet was bigger around than Jupiter with over twice its mass. Material poured off the star and swirled around the planet in a great whirlpool.

"It's like a maelstrom to Hell itself," breathed Suki.

"Welcome to Kepler-17b," said the captain from the front of the battle deck. He turned around and saw that Roberts aimed a gun at Suki. "What's going on?"

"I found her with the device we brought aboard," said Roberts. "She could be working with our pursuers."

"Why?" asked the captain.

"To get passage back to Earth," suggested the first mate.

The captain shook his head. "The agent we were picking up was from Earth. Wherever our pursuers are from, it's a long way in some other direction." Despite the surety of his words, Firebrandt's eyes darted toward Computer. "Any unauthorized communications the last few days?

"Negative," said Computer. "But, pursuing ships are now in weapons' range."

A moment later, the ship rocked as it was hit by a high-energy pulse from one of the ships. Roberts fought to control his balance, then holstered his pistol and stepped forward to his station.

"Whatever it is we have," said Firebrandt around the pipe stem, "they would rather destroy it than let it fall into someone else's hands."

"They must have another," said Roberts.

"You know what it is, then?" asked the captain.

"I have an idea, but it's pretty hard to believe."

The ship shuddered again. At that point, the image in the holographic tank began to break up. Enough of the image was still visible to tell they were heading into the material flowing from the star to the planet.

"We're encountering sensory interference. I won't be able to keep the display in the holographic tank," reported Computer. A moment later, the image dissolved and faded away like a clearing fog.

Roberts peered at his console. "It's hard to get a reading on the pursuing ships, but it looks like they've slowed. They're not going to follow us."

"That's good, and if we can't see them, they can't see us." Firebrandt nodded. "How long can we stay here?"

Roberts shook his head. "Not long. Hull temperature is already climbing to dangerous levels. I'm guessing we have four or five hours at maximum."

"So, what exactly did you find out about our cargo?" asked Firebrandt.

Roberts explained what Suki described. "It looks like it's designed to connect into a star vessel's engine and generate a jump point on the spot."

Firebrandt's bushy red eyebrows lifted. "Do you think we could make it work with our engines?"

Roberts sat back and folded his arms. "Balancing the power would be the real challenge. Too little and it won't do anything. Too much and it'll scatter our molecules throughout the cosmos." He took a deep breath and let it out slowly. "I could probably manage it with time, but it's not the way out of our current dilemma."

Suki stepped between Firebrandt and Roberts. "I think I could make it work in two or three hours."

Firebrandt took the pipe from his mouth and Roberts scowled.

She shrugged. "The interface looked pretty straightforward."

They continued to stare at her.

She planted her fists on her hips. "Look, I taught hyperspatial dynamics on Prospero. I can do this, especially if Mr. Roberts gives me a hand with the programming."

Firebrandt nodded slowly and placed the pipe back in his mouth. "Can you leave my engines intact so we can get out of here in a hurry if we need to?

Suki thought about that for a minute. "At most, we'd need them down for fifteen minutes while we hook up power couplings."

"Let me know before you disable anything. If it won't work, leave well enough alone. I like the possibilities this gadget presents, but I'm not going to count on it."

Suki swallowed and nodded. "Understood." She looked back at Roberts who surprised her by nodding thoughtfully.

"It's certainly worth a look. We'll see what we can do." He stood and ushered Suki back into the corridor. She followed him to a storage room where they retrieved an anti-gravity cart, then returned to the device abandoned in the corridor. He lowered the cart to the deck. The silence and tension had grown palpable by the time she helped him roll the device onto the cart. "I really don't understand what you're doing here," said Roberts as he activated the cart again.

Suki wasn't really sure how to answer. She wasn't sure what she was doing there, either. "Why are *you* here, Mr. Roberts?"

He reached up and rubbed his bald head. For the first time, she really looked at him closely. She noticed the subtle telltales of reconstructive surgery. The first mate had once been injured badly. "I've witnessed true evil, Ms. Suki. It wore gray uniforms and no insignias."

She shuddered, remembering Bowman's soldiers of fortune. "Were these the men that ambushed you at the space station?"

He took a deep breath and let it out slowly. "I suppose so

... but I'm thinking of other places and other times. Such men require numbers for bravery. Their employers think money buys them power." He looked into her eyes. "Such men try to rule the galaxy, Ms. Suki. They would have us all wear gray uniforms and be dutiful soldiers in their cause." Without further comment, he pushed the cart toward the engine room.

* * *

Two hours later, Captain Firebrandt stood on the battle deck staring at a holographic representation of the Kepler-17 system. The *Legacy* was shown between the spotted star and the gas giant in the flow of material between the two bodies. The ship sat in the Lagrange point, traveling around the star every hour and a half with the planet. With no external sensors, the two pursuing ships were not visible. There was a rumbling sound, and the deck seemed to drop out from under the captain's feet for a moment as the walls shuddered. Firebrandt took the pipe from his mouth. "What the hell was that?"

"By the magnitude of the disturbance, I'd say a high energy discharge," reported Computer.

"From the star?" asked the captain.

"More likely, it was a discharge from an external source. We felt it because of the density of the material around us."

"Damn! They're taking pot shots at us, hoping to get lucky." He stepped over to Roberts's console and checked the diagnostics screen. They were running out of time, faster than he liked. What was almost worse, the hull was hot and covered in charged particles. When they emerged, they would be glowing in just about every possible wavelength.

Another rumble passed through the ship, weaker than the first. A smile spread across the captain's face. "I have an idea about how to get out of here."

"Captain," said Roberts from the intercom, before he could voice his idea.

"Go ahead." Firebrandt set his pipe down on the console.

"Suki and I have programs ready to load into our engine controllers and we're ready to hook in the nodal-point generator," reported the first mate.

"Warning!" Computer's voice rang out. "The power consumption for our shields and cooling is dangerously high. We only have battery reserves for five minutes. We cannot disengage main power longer or we'll lose our ability to maintain position."

"Did you hear that?" asked the captain.

"Five minutes should be more than enough time," said Roberts.

Firebrandt leaned close to the intercom. "I think I have a way out of here that won't need the generator. I'm not sure if we should risk it."

"Captain," interrupted Suki. "I was conservative allocating power to the device. In the worst case, this thing just won't work. Installing it won't prevent the engines working normally."

"She's got a point," said Roberts. "Better to go into the next match holding as many cards as possible."

The ship shuddered again, causing Firebrandt's pipe to clatter to the deck. "All right, let's get it done in four minutes."

As Firebrandt reached over to pick up the pipe and stamp out the glowing ash, the lights dimmed and the holographic display of Kepler-17 winked out. The mechanics had cut main power. The captain rotated in the seat to face Computer. "Let me know if any systems approach critical."

"Yes, sir." Computer's eyes slowly scanned back and forth as he carefully monitored ship's systems.

The captain stood and loaded more tobacco into his pipe. He lit it as he paced toward the stern of the battle deck. Nicole Lowry sat at the engineering console, monitoring Roberts's and Suki's progress.

"Stand by at the starboard gunner's rig," ordered the captain. "Get Martinez up here to take port. As soon as main power's back on, bring the weapons on line and stand by."

Lowry nodded and called Cesar Martinez to the battle deck. Firebrandt turned and paced back toward the inactive holographic display, only briefly losing his footing when another jolt hit the ship. He loosened the top two buttons of his jacket and wiped sweat from his brow.

"Battery reserves down to one minute," stated Computer.

As Firebrandt turned toward Roberts's console, Martinez entered the battle deck and joined Lowry by the gunner's rigs.

The captain sat down and activated the intercom. "We're running out of time."

Instead of responding, the lights brightened. The captain let out a sigh of relief.

"It's looking good," said Roberts from the intercom. "We'll be up in a minute."

Firebrandt stood and noted both the satisfying rumble of the main engines and the whine of the weapons systems coming on line. Roberts and Suki appeared on the battle deck a few minutes later.

"So, what do you have for me? Can we jump out of here?" asked the captain.

Suki shook her head. "We're too close to the bottom of the system's gravitational well. We're going to need some distance before we can try a jump."

"What's more," added Roberts, "we won't be able to jump to a different system. The device only lets us make a brief jump. A timer controls our reentry into normal space. I'm guessing our maximum range using the device is a few hundred million kilometers."

Firebrandt nodded. "That might be useful. If it fails, can we switch back to main engines?"

Suki gave a curt nod.

The captain eyed her for a moment, then removed the pipe from his mouth and saw that he had smoked through the tobacco. He placed the pipe in his pocket and cleared his throat. "All right, here's the plan. We're going to spin around, firing bursts with the main pulse cannon and the turret guns. Those ships, whoever they are, are looking for something hot to come out of here. We'll give them something hot! Once we've finished our spin, we'll blast out of here and begin scanning as soon as we can." He looked toward Computer. "Do we have a jump point to a safe harbor?"

"There is one. I have approximate position on record. I'll fine tune the position as soon as sensors are on line again."

"That's good enough. Send that position to el-Din." The captain smiled. "Get in positions everyone, this is sure to be a hell of a ride."

Firebrandt grabbed the railing near the holographic tank.

Roberts crossed to his station and Suki strapped herself into the seat Nicole Lowry had vacated earlier. She brought up the command system for the nodal-point generator.

"Let's make this happen." With that, the captain tightened his grip on the rail. The helmsman activated the thrusters and everyone was thrown toward the starboard wall as the ship began its spin. Thundering bursts sounded as the main pulse gun fired, punctuated by the staccato of the turret guns. In the holographic tank, the ship could be seen pirouetting between the planet and the star. Hot spots flared out in all directions, many falling rapidly into Kepler-17. The captain pointed to el-Din. "Get us out of here!"

The helmsman activated the controls and the ship shot out of its hiding place. The captain ground his teeth as he waited for the sensors to come back on line, giving him a real picture of what was going on around the ship.

The computer model soon dissolved into the real view in front of the ship. The captain thought he saw something glimmering in their path. "Computer, enhance! What's that?"

The view in the holographic tank snapped into a close-up view of one of the mysterious vessels that had been pursuing them. It was firing thrusters, bringing its main gun to bear on their position.

"Crap!" He turned around and pointed at Suki. "Let's hope this nodal point generator works!"

The enemy ship's forward gun began glowing as she typed. A cone showing the ship's estimated firing vector was displayed in the hologram. "They're in firing range," declared Roberts.

"Ready," declared Suki.

"Jump!" ordered the captain.

At first, nothing happened.

Suki spun around, her eyes scanning the displays. Without a word, she began typing again.

"What's going on?" asked Firebrandt.

"We have a slight imbalance," said Suki. "I'm adjusting."

"Enemy ship has fired main pulse gun," reported Computer.

Firebrandt pointed to el-Din, "Evasive…"

"Jumping," said Suki.

The captain felt the deck drop out from beneath his feet. He slammed his eyes shut against the strange sounds the engine made and, without thinking, he slammed his hands over his ears to shut out the sights of his ship swirling just beyond the reach of normal space. A moment later, reality came back into focus and Firebrandt found himself sprawled on the deck, his shoulder screaming in pain. The unmistakable slosh and splatter of someone emptying their stomach sounded from astern.

Firebrandt sat up. "Get this holo live again!"

An image appeared in the holographic tank. An empty star field lay ahead.

"Pan around the ship," ordered the captain. "Where are we, exactly?"

As the view shifted, they saw they had jumped just beyond one of the two warships. They were looking right at the glowing engine.

"Turret guns," called the captain, "fire into their engines! Buy us some time!"

Nicole Lowry fired several bursts. One burst knocked out the pursuing ship's thrusters. Another took out their main EQ engine. The explosion sent the enemy ship hurtling toward Kepler-17.

"Jump point in one minute," announced Kheir el-Din.

"Number two vessel has stopped pursuit and is moving in to assist its companion," reported Computer.

"Excellent," said Firebrandt. "Everyone, prepare for jump. This place is getting too hot for me."

* * *

That evening, Suki returned to her cabin and took a shower. The warm water relaxed her muscles and began to ease away the tensions of the day. She wondered what was next. Perhaps the captain would be sufficiently grateful for her help that she could ask to be dropped at an Earth colony with enough credits to buy passage home. It was a pleasant thought. She turned off the water, stepped from the shower and toweled off.

In the main room, she saw a message flashing on her tablet. The captain had invited her to his cabin for dinner. She sighed, not really sure she wanted to spend more time with the pirates, but food sounded good. She dressed and went to the captain's cabin.

She found both the captain and first mate there when she arrived. Firebrandt turned to him. "Mr. Roberts, do you still have any doubts that Suki was working with the people pursuing us?"

The first mate shook his head. "I don't see how she could. What's more, we need her skills with this new device aboard."

"That's exactly what I was thinking." The captain reached over and activated a button on his intercom console. A moment later, the ship's cook, Juan de Largo appeared at the door with a cart. He set out Suki's favorite meal, yakitori. The captain looked at her and narrowed his gaze. "Suki, we need you to be more than a passenger. Are you willing to help us?"

She swallowed and considered Roberts's words about soldiers in gray uniforms. Perhaps there needed to be a little chaos in the form of pirates to keep even worse villains at bay. "I'm not sure how I feel about being a pirate, sir, but I do find the device fascinating."

The captain poured a glass of South African wine and lifted it in a toast. "To our newest crewmember. Long may she keep our fat out of the fire."

Roberts poured a glass for Suki, then one for himself and he held it up. The captain and first mate drank and sat down.

After taking a drink, Suki sat at the table. "So, what do we do now?"

"Sitting between that star and planet, then attaching an untested new device into our engine, we fried a few systems," said Roberts. "I think we're going to want to sit tight for a little while and make repairs."

"I agree," said the captain. "Besides, we could do with a break before we figure out our next move."

Suki blinked. "What about the nodal point generator? Clearly the agent you met was stealing it to take it back to Earth."

"But which agency? Did they even know we were involved?" Firebrandt shrugged. "Quite honestly, I think that device is worth more to me right where it is than any payment we'd get from Earth."

"But what if they notice you have it and come looking?" Suki's eyebrows came together.

Roberts sat back and folded his arms. "Secrets like this are pretty fleeting and I suspect we don't have the only prototype in existence, but she has a point. Someone may decide the easiest way to get one of these units is to try and take ours."

Firebrandt picked up his chopsticks and began rubbing them together. "Ms. Suki, do you think you could build me a second generator?"

"I'd have to spend time getting to know the one we have."

The captain nodded. "That's exactly what I'd like you to do."

Suki leaned forward. "But why do you want a second generator?"

"If someone comes looking, we'll have one to give them."

She smiled as she rubbed her chopsticks together. "I can't wait to begin."

Kepler-4

Kepler-4 is a star slightly larger and hotter than our sun. It hosts a planet much like Neptune in size. Too bad it is a roaster … a very close-in planet that is terribly hot. However, it might be a lovely place for a vacation and just about right for barbeque. So, forget Warp Drive and ride along with Elaine and her friends for a really fast trip across the galaxy. Just make sure you pack enough for a long stay away…

Kepler-4	Stellar Characteristics
Temperature	5857 Kelvins
Mass	1.2 Solar masses
Radius	1.5 Solar radii
Visual magnitude	12
Distance from Earth	1793 Light years

Kepler-4b	Planet Characteristics
Temperature	1650 Kelvins
Mass	24.5 Earth masses
Radius	4.0 Earth radii
Orbital Period	3.2 days
Distance from Star	0.05 AUs

Tracking the Glints
Anna Paradox

All vision glared to white; all sound rose to a screaming crescendo of noise. Elaine Mar felt pressed into her acceleration sling, then pressed everywhere, even from within. Then they were through, and thousands of invisible fingers retreated gram by gram.

Her ears were still ringing. She shook her head—she always did—and still it was long breaths before her vision faded in again, and she could see the gauges before her, and Dave Grandin to her left. Behind her, she heard the small rustlings as Cormac Halloran and Javier Chavez shifted in their slings.

She read the gauges in checklist order. "Pressure nominal. Fuel level as predicted. Velocity nominal. Exterior integrity ... holding. Solar spectrum ... as predicted."

"We made it again," said Dave.

After a moment, they broke into a ragged cheer. Eight times. Eight times, they'd made it through a glint. They'd visited eight solar systems since leaving Earth—maybe the most any humans had, even yet.

"I wonder if we are anywhere near home," said Cormac.

"Let's find out. We have work to do, folks," said Dave.

And so Elaine released her restraints and walked unsteadily from the command module. *The gardens first,* she thought. There'd be time for the welding when she had her acceleration legs again.

* * *

Javier found her frowning at a seed bed. She looked up at the strong, dark planes of his face. "What news?"

"The good news is we know where we are. Kepler-4b is in tight orbit around its sun. You'll want to get a look at it."

"All right." Blue eyes regarded him a moment, then she turned back to crumble a bit of soil between slender fingers. "And the bad news?"

"We're over sixteen hundred light years from Earth. It just doesn't make sense. You'd think with ten data points, we'd have a pattern by now. I really thought this last glint would take us closer to home. But—"

"But here we are." She brushed dirt off her fingers and wrapped an arm around him. "No one's blaming you."

"I'm blaming me! Look, we know each glint leads from one star system to another, and back. We ran dozens of probes back and forth through the three in Sol system. Always goes to the same place, always comes back. But the direction and distance—there has to be a pattern, and I can't find it."

"Maybe their alien makers had a strange sense of humor. Or they mainly wanted to silence our radio waves."

"Nice try, babe. We know they have to be a natural phenomenon—if only because an intelligent race wouldn't be able to resist signing them."

Elaine's lips quirked at the old argument. "Maybe they're minimalists."

"Nope. No way." He shrugged loose from her arm to point a blunt finger at the seed bed. "What's going on here?"

Elaine brushed sandy hair from her cheek. "I can't get any more tomato seeds to germinate. I'm going to miss spaghetti sauce."

"Ouch. Me too." They both gazed at the empty plant tray. "I really thought this last glint would take us closer to home. But here we are, farther from Earth than ever. Do you think we should turn back?"

Elaine looked up, pale eyes meeting dark ones. There hadn't been those wrinkles at the corners of Javier's eyes when they left Sol system. "I don't know," she said. "How many glints do we have to choose from here?"

"I've spotted one so far, plus the one we came through. Give me a few days, and I'll give you a better answer."

She nodded. "Same here."

* * *

The few days after passing through a glint were always the busiest on the *Pegasus*. Everyone took turns, cooking, doing maintenance, and cleaning. Javier, the primary astrophysicist, mapped extra-system items and searched for glints. Cormac tracked in-system items, and searched for the mass and elements they'd need to fuel the ship and supply the compositor. Dave piloted and plotted courses, capturing an icy comet and a metallic one.

Elaine was the life specialist—a xenobiologist largely work-ing as a gardener, since they had yet to find any extra-solar life. Over eighteen years, she'd saved seeds and replanted, and kept them fed, and never lost a crop—until the tomatoes.

She'd give it one more try. She pressed seeds into the soil, and watered them. No point in staying to watch them.

As she left the garden bay, she thought about the subtle dif-ference between a completely sustainable system and a most-ly sustainable system. Were the tomatoes a fluke, or the first wedge of the collapse of the garden?

* * *

She found Cormac at the compositor, fingers pounding the keyboard of the code interface, feet tapping out a count-er-rhythm. She took the other chair and waited. Twenty min-utes passed before he paused, looked around, and saw her.

"Elaine!" He rose and hugged her. "I kept meaning to find you!"

"Here I am," she said. "The garden's all in order, so I thought I'd see if you needed a hand replating the hull."

"Always, always." He blinked grey eyes at her. His hair, once bright red, was faded now with grey strands mixed throughout. "Great timing. I'm almost ready to go out. I've just been reprogramming the steel plate mix. We're running low on vanadium."

"Is that critical?" Elaine asked.

"No, the steel will still work. It's just a little less optimal than the original mix."

They walked around to the dispensing end of the compos-itor. Given the right mix of elements as inputs and a careful-ly programmed recipe, it could build just about anything that wasn't too complex. In practice, "not too complex" meant any-thing manufactured from simple compounds but not anything that had been alive. The compositor renewed the *Pegasus'* me-chanical systems the same way Elaine's seed saving renewed the gardens.

A steel sheet, one meter square, dropped into the output box, and another began to emerge.

"How's the compositor doing?"

Cormac patted the side of the box. "She's still running like a charm. Not a hitch in eighteen years, eh, my beauty?"

"So we are good to keep going?"

He rounded on her, face hardening. "Now that, I didn't say. We need to head back." He thumped the compositor, hard enough for the sound to ring throughout the mechanics bay. "This machine might outlast us all. But I am getting tired."

Elaine held up her hands. "Okay, okay."

He let his shoulders fall. "Elaine. You know it's not you I'm mad at. You have to convince Dave to let us turn back. He'll listen to you."

"Javier thought we might find a shorter route home."

"And he was wrong, wasn't he? He has no idea where the next glint will take us. Our only choice is to retrace our steps, and hope we haven't left that too long."

Elaine took a breath. "Do you think we have?"

"I heard about the tomatoes," Cormac said. "But even without that—I feel the ship getting more fragile around me. I feel us getting more strained—we hardly talk to each other any more. The ship is big—and it isn't normal for humans to spend days without coming near other humans."

"I'll talk to Dave. And we can all have dinner together tonight."

"You're a good girl, Elaine." He put his arm around her. "I hear that you haven't said you'll ask him to turn around. But I know you'll do the right thing."

"I'll do what I know is right. And I haven't decided yet."

"Fair enough. Come on, let's suit up and patch the hull. The sights are particularly good in this system."

* * *

They worked in the lee of the ship, placing a new layer of plate over the *Pegasus'* hull. Each time they entered a system, they cut from one glint to another near the edge of a new star's gravity sway. They'd grab a few rocks, take many pictures, and push to a significant fraction of c. Even rare specks of dust, at one-half the speed of light, add up to significant hull abrasion. They'd spent from one to three years in each system. In theory, as long as they placed a new layer on the hull in each system, the *Pegasus* could fly on forever.

That was, if the crew lived forever to apply the patches.

This time, Elaine and Cormac worked at the edge of a yellow star system. Their faceplates filtered out harmful radiation, so they could look towards Kepler-4, and watch the planet, Kepler-4b, cross it. From just over 40AUs away, there was just enough disk to see a black dot crossing it. Elaine dialed up the magnification.

A band of multicolored gases shimmered around Kepler-4's equator. They bled off from the closely orbiting planet, and lingered, an iridescent belt around the star, glowing against the black background of space.

"This is a beautiful system," Elaine said.

Cormac replied over the short range suit radio. "It is. One of the first extra-solar planets discovered by Earth astronomers—one hundred and twenty-six years ago."

"This is what makes an eighteen year voyage worth it."

"Do you think so? Then we'd better go back to Earth and tell them about it."

She didn't reply. After an hour of silence and welding, they'd attached the day's stack of steel sheets, and they went back inside.

* * *

Elaine dropped her spacesuit in a specialized compositor for cleaning, testing, and returning to spec. She lingered a little over combing her hair and freshening her clothes. Talking to Dave was always hardest.

She found him on the flight deck. He turned and ran a hand through his rich brown hair when he heard her enter. She used to love that hair.

"Hello, Elaine. What brings you to Mission Control?"

"I came to invite you to dinner. I'm making lasagna."

"Sounds good." He gazed at her a little while longer, then turned back to the viewscreens. "Javier has found us four glints to choose from. It's probably time we discuss which one we're going to take next."

"What about the one we came out of?"

"Are you going to turn against me, too?"

"I'm not against you, Dave. I'm just saying, that one might need to be on our menu."

He kept his back to her, and shook his head. "We're farther from Earth than anyone has ever been. I'd like to see a little more."

She stepped forward to lay a hand on his shoulder. "Dave. How far are we going to go?"

"As far as you'll let me."

She dropped her hand. "Cormac's worried. Javier's losing hope. The ship could make it—I'm not sure we can."

"I'm not doing this just for me, Elaine. Those kids we left behind—they'll get a million for every system we visit. It's the least we could do for them."

"We could go back to them."

He glared at her in frustration. "They'll be grandparents by the time we come back. What good will we be to them?"

"They won't even get the money if Earth doesn't hear where we've been. How do you propose to let them know? Even if radio could cross the glint barrier, it would take over sixteen hundred years to reach home."

"We'll send an automated probe back. I'm sure I can program one to retrace our steps. That will work."

"We'd never know!" Elaine heard her voice rising, and made herself stop. "Dave, I don't want to fight with you. We all need to talk, and find what our best choice is here."

"I know which way the wind is blowing! The three of you are going to vote to turn back. Fine. That overrides my captain's decision, as we agreed so long ago. I never thought you'd go against me."

"Dave, don't you want to see Earth again?"

"What happened to you and me, exploring together, to the ends of the galaxy? Don't you miss me?"

Elaine closed her eyes. "I do, sometimes. It's just so hard ... you feel strange to me. I feel strange to myself." She opened her eyes, and found him standing face to face with her. "I think that's what worries Cormac the most. These wide open spaces—they're changing us."

"Then be with me, just for a little while. For old time's sake. I'm the only authority around, and I still haven't granted us a divorce."

The sound Elaine made was somewhere between a laugh

and a sob. She let him pull her against him.

* * *

Elaine went to the kitchen by herself an hour before dinner. She pulled the next-to-last container of tomato sauce out of the freezer, busied herself in the ritual of lasagna. Although they secured their goods against the possibility of freefall, by clever combinations of spin and acceleration, most of the *Pegasus* seemed to have gravity, most of the time. It made many tasks simpler.

Dave arrived just before the others. He kissed her cheek as he came in. "Do what you must," he said. She smiled at him, then brought dishes to the table as Cormac and Javier took their places.

They ate first. Everyone complimented her on the food. Then, plates empty, they sat, reluctant to end a peaceful moment.

Delay wouldn't help. Elaine gathered herself to start.

But Dave spoke first. "Javier, tell us about the glints here."

Javier spread his dark, broad hands palm up on the table. "I've found four, in addition to the one we came through. The closest is a red, spinwise ahead of us. Behind us, the yellow we came from, then another yellow. Across the system, another yellow and a blue white."

"That's good news to take home," said Cormac. "Every time we've gone through a glint, it's led to a star that matched the glint's spectrum. It's time we left glints for someone else to explore."

"What if we went to each glint, jumped through to see where it led, and then came back? We could complete the whole circuit, and then go home," said Dave.

Cormac groaned. "Come on, Dave. In the first systems, I suggested that, and you didn't want to do it, since the people following us could check out the ones close to home. Well, now, I don't want to do it. It will take us at least six years to complete the circuit, and probably twelve, with all the rocks we'll need to catch. I'm not willing to wait that long. I'm too old to wait three more decades to get home."

"Javier? Wouldn't four more data points help you find the pattern?" asked Dave.

Javier rolled his eyes to the ceiling. "If ten points hasn't done it, fourteen isn't going to do it. I don't think there is a pattern." He straightened. "I want to go home, too."

"That's two," said Dave. "Elaine?"

She looked at him, then looked around the table, to find Cormac and Javier's attention fixed on her as well. "Wait," she said. "Wait, there has to be something.... Javier, are you sure there's no pattern?"

He shrugged. "It has me beat, Elaine. I don't see a thing."

"Please, let's go through this again. If we all try ... what is everything we know about the glints?"

"What's the use?" asked Javier.

Cormac covered one of Javier's hands with his own. "Let's give it an hour. After all this time, we can spare an hour to work on this together. Show us the map, Javier."

"All right."

They dimmed the lights. Javier projected a galactic map above the table.

"I've enlarged the systems here, to show the glints. So systems are too large on the scale of the map. But the distances between systems is to scale."

"Okay," said Elaine. "So what do we know?"

"All the glints hover at the edge of their systems. They fall on a circle, where the gravity of the sun is just losing its primacy over the combined forces from outside the system."

"Add another piece to take home," said Cormac. "Glints always orbit at the edge of the system."

"No," said Javier. "That's not quite right. They don't orbit. You could say they are in an orbit, I guess, but they don't circle their star. They are fixed relative to the galactic background instead."

"So they should fall towards the star," said Dave.

"And they don't. That's one of the reasons I thought they must have a pattern. Why would they stay fixed against the galactic background if their position had no relation to where they connected to? But maybe it's just because they don't have any mass, so gravity doesn't affect them."

"Show me how they connect," said Elaine.

"Okay." Javier drew three lines out from the three glints

at the edge of Sol system. "From Earth, you can go here, here, or here. This system's 38 light years away, this one's 52, and this one's 116. We took the middle one. Only two glints in that system, so we took the new one. See how they both point away from the system's sun, when you project a line from the glint to the system it reaches. I thought we had the start of a pattern there. That jump was 61, and they weren't quite on a line. Then the next one blew that idea to pieces."

He drew three more lines in quick succession. "So next we wanted to see if glint color matched star color. So we hit a red sun, a blue-white sun, and another red sun, and that works. But look at this. We'd been zig-zagging away from Earth, and then we suddenly jumped 457 light years, by far the longest jump yet, and found ourselves most of the way back towards home."

"We were only 68 light years away," said Cormac. "If radio wasn't scrambled at the glint radius, we could have heard base-ball games. We could have sent a probe back the slow way, and they might still remember who we are when it arrived."

Dave frowned. "I told you, I can get a probe to go back through the glints. We won't have to send it the slow way."

"You need to put in some time on the hull after we go through," said Cormac.

"Wait," said Elaine. "That's our first six glints. What happened on these last two?"

Javier drew two more lines. "Once again, I thought I might see a pattern. That longest jump was from a system that was relatively isolated. See how it has few neighbors? So I thought maybe the distance related to the density of stars from the system. And the next one kind of fit that pattern. Then this last one—blew that to pieces, too."

"And sent us the farthest from Earth yet," said Cormac. "We've clearly gone the wrong way. It's time to go home."

"Fine," said Dave. "Shall we vote now?"

"Hang on!" said Elaine. "There has to be more. I'm not ready to vote."

"What else is there to say?" asked Javier.

"Elaine, you don't have to wait just to spare my feelings," said Dave.

"It's not that," she said. "I keep feeling there's something else. What about the radio wave effect, Javier? Doesn't that make it look like someone intelligent built these things?"

He shook his head. "Just a coincidence. When radio waves reach the glint radius, some of them are shifted out of phase, and they cancel each other out. It's all random. So if you have a complex signal, like music, it mostly interferes with itself, and not much gets out. Anything with a message tends to go the same way. Strong, simple signals would have an easier time getting through. Or maybe pulsars are even louder than we think."

"They sure haven't made themselves obvious," said Cormac. "I'd think they'd want to talk."

"I'd think they want us to come find them," said Dave.

Elaine traced the lines with her index finger. "Javier, what do you mean, fixed with respect to the galactic background? Isn't the galaxy moving?"

"Sure, but slow, compared to how fast the glints would orbit if they were circling their stars. And they do move, a little..."

"Show me. How do they move?"

"Ok, here's a star, and here's a glint, and here's the galaxy. The glint moves..." Suddenly Javier started rearranging the systems. "Huhn. With the star it connects to. So if we make three copies of the Earth system, and we pile all the stars on top of each other, and rotate all the systems so that all the glints are in the same place..."

It was as if all the lines resolved into the shape of a chambered nautilus.

"Holy shit," said Javier. "The pattern."

"You did it!" said Dave. He grabbed Elaine and kissed her full on the lips.

All the stars lay on a perfect spiral, circling out from the glint and around the system. Most were on the first circuit, two were on the second circuit, and the last two had a circuit to themselves.

"That's why I couldn't see it," said Javier. "Distance does relate to angle, but if you go beyond a certain point, it circles around again. So these two glints, with big differences in length, have almost the same angle..."

"Another twenty glints, and you'd have gotten it, easy," said Dave.

Elaine poked his shoulder. "Dave!"

Cormac leaned over the table. "Does this mean we can tell where the glints go?"

Javier considered. "Maybe. We have two pieces of information. We know the color of the star, and the shape of the spiral. If there's only one star of that color on the spiral, we have it."

"We have a third piece of information. The rate the glints are moving at," said Dave.

"So if we can't tell at first, we might know in a few months. Yeah."

"So, let's see where we can go from here," said Cormac.

"Right, right." Javier grabbed the spiral, erased the lines, pulled their current system to the center of the table. "Here's the one we came through." He copied the spiral from it extending over the galactic map. "And there's the system we came from, right on the spiral. It works backwards too."

"Since the glint could be anywhere on the exterior radius," said Dave.

"Yeah." Erasing that spiral, Javier moved onto the next glint spinward around the system. The spiral shot out from it—and only intersected one star, a red one matching the color of the glint.

"Oh, that's nice!" said Elaine.

Javier's fingers picked up speed. Two stars on the next spiral, but only one matched color. One star on the fourth spiral. One star on the fifth spiral, and...

"I know that system," said Dave. "Isn't that?"

"Sol," said Javier.

"Earth my boy! Earth!" said Cormac, pounding Javier on the back.

"I vote for that one," said Elaine.

"This isn't one of the glints we know in Earth's system. But they are hard to see," said Javier.

"Or maybe the aliens just put it there. For us," said Elaine.

"Let's go find out," said Dave.

* * *

They flew the *Pegasus* anti-spinward for five months. Her inhabitants ate together more often, and smiled more often. They egged each other on to test more g's of acceleration for longer periods.

And then Dave slotted the *Pegasus* into the glint. All space went white, in vision and noise, and thousands of invisible fingers pressed upon them. Elaine shook her head, as she always did, and vision came back.

She started to read the gauges, then said, "Can you hear me? I still have white noise."

Dave twisted to grin at her. "That's not white noise! It's radio. I turned it on before we went through."

And he accelerated the *Pegasus* inside the glint radius, and they dove for home with all the music and voices of Earth coming through loud and clear.

Kepler-11

Ah, the king of the Kepler planetary systems, so far. Kepler-11 has six orbiting planets discovered to date. All of them orbit their sun-like star closer than our planet Venus. In fact, the planets are so tightly packed together that they gravitationally interact with each other. With so many planets, one might not expect this system to be a lonely place—however a sort of eighteenth century Australia comes to mind. Limbo conjures up visions to last a long, long time.

Kepler-11	Stellar Characteristics
Temperature	5680 Kelvins
Mass	0.95 Solar masses
Radius	1.1 Solar radii
Visual magnitude	14
Distance from Earth	1998 Light years

Kepler-11b	Planet Characteristics
Temperature	900 Kelvins
Mass	4.3 Earth masses
Radius	2.0 Earth radii
Orbital Period	10 days
Distance from Star	0.09 AUs

Kepler-11c	Planet Characteristics
Temperature	833 Kelvins
Mass	13.5 Earth masses
Radius	3.2 Earth radii
Orbital Period	13 days
Distance from Star	0.11 AUs

Continued on next page.

Kepler-11d	Planet Characteristics
Temperature	692 Kelvins
Mass	6.1 Earth masses
Radius	3.4 Earth radii
Orbital Period	22.7 days
Distance from Star	0.16 AUs

Kepler-11e	Planet Characteristics
Temperature	617 Kelvins
Mass	8.4 Earth masses
Radius	4.5 Earth radii
Orbital Period	32 days
Distance from Star	0.19 AUs

Kepler-11f	Planet Characteristics
Temperature	544 Kelvins
Mass	2.3 Earth masses
Radius	2.6 Earth radii
Orbital Period	46.7 days
Distance from Star	0.25 AUs

Kepler-11g	Planet Characteristics
Temperature	400 Kelvins
Mass	>35 Earth masses
Radius	3.7 Earth radii
Orbital Period	118 days
Distance from Star	0.46 AUs

An Eternity in Limbo
J Alan Erwine

The swirling clouds of Kepler-11f boiled and bubbled be-neath Space Station Argos. Kepler-11f was the official designa-tion for the planet that the scientists used, but it wasn't what most of the space station's inhabitants called the planet. To them, it was Limbo, which was pretty much the state they all found themselves in.

Space Station Argos had been put in orbit of Kepler-11f more than a decade earlier so that the scientists could research the planet, and the other planets in the Kepler-11 system, but the people who actually did all of the grunt work on the station weren't scientists. Instead, they were prisoners, but not prison-ers like most people would think.

Adam Jenkins was one of those prisoners, but he wasn't a murder, or a rapist, or even a petty thief. No, his crime was much worse in the eyes of the government. He was a political dissident, and for his unpopular views of the government, he now found himself spending ten years orbiting a broiling gas giant in a tin can doing all of the dirty work for the scientists who had the full support of the government because they pret-ty much did whatever the government told them to do.

"One day closer to freedom," he said, completely unable to keep the sarcasm out of his voice. He lay back in his favorite chair in the common room, stretching his long legs out and putting them up on the table in front of him.

"Yeah," William Harrington mumbled. "One day closer, but how many still to go?" he asked, his voice slowly rising.

Adam chose to ignore him. Harrington had never been one of his favorite people. He had a bad attitude that often seemed contagious. Granted, it was hard to have a good attitude when you were more or less a prisoner, but Adam was getting used to it, and there was no way he was going to spend the remaining six years of his sentence moping around.

"How many to go?" Harrington asked again.

Adam sighed. Most of the time, ignoring Harrington would keep him from talking, but apparently this wasn't going to be one of those times. "About six years," Adam said. "You do the math on the days if you really want to."

Whereas Adam was almost six and a half feet tall, Harrington was a short man, maybe five and a half feet tall if he stretched. He had a small goatee, a bit of a pot-belly, and thinning blonde hair. It was obvious he was a bright guy, but he never really talked like it. He acted more like a real criminal than a political criminal, but that didn't really matter to Adam. He'd already spent way too much time thinking about Harrington.

"Too many. That's all I know," a voice boomed from the doorway. Adam didn't have to turn to know it was Lenny Bishop. Lenny had a voice that probably echoed all the way back to Earth, even through the vacuum of space.

Adam thought of Harrington as a sniveling weasel, but Lenny was an outgoing, life-of-the-party type, that Adam had taken an instant liking to. He was tall, almost as tall as Adam, but Lenny was also quite rotund, massing close to 300 pounds, but the low gravity of Station Argos was a blessing for Lenny, who could get around almost as easily as everyone else.

Adam and Harrington were political prisoners, but Lenny was something much worse, at least worse on Station Argos. He was a former scientist who had been caught falsifying data, or at least that's what the conviction records show. Lenny said that the data was accurate, but the government didn't like the data, so they nailed him to the wall and sent him to Limbo.

"You'll probably never get out of here," Adam said with a laugh. It struck most people as odd, but Adam and Lenny actually had a good time together, even though they were prisoners ... of a sort.

"That's for sure," Harrington added, trying to laugh along with the other two, but they both stopped laughing. It didn't seem all that funny anymore.

"Can't you ever stay out of a conversation, Willy?" Lenny asked, using the nickname that Harrington hated. Everyone on the station knew that the two didn't like each other.

Harrington just stared daggers back at Lenny.

"Adam Jenkins to Observation Pod B immediately," a voice chimed over the intercom.

"Hate to leave you boys in the middle of such an intellectually stimulating conversation, but duty calls," Adam said, standing up and leaving the other two still staring at each other.

* * *

Adam hated being a prisoner, but there were times when he really loved his work, and when he was called to Observation Pod B, he knew he was in for a good couple of hours. OPB had one of the best views of Limbo on the entire station. From his seat next to Dr. Yamamoto, he could see the hydrogen clouds below him bubble and churn, mixing orange, white, and yellow into new colors he never could have predicted. Adam had grown up on Earth, and before he'd become political, he'd toured the solar system, including visiting Ganymede. From there he'd watched the clouds of Jupiter, and he'd been mesmerized, but Limbo was much hotter than Jupiter since it was so much closer to its sun, and this caused weather, and thus the cloud movement to be so much faster and more dynamic than anything Jupiter could ever hope to conjure.

"Adam," Dr. Yamamoto said.

"Yeah," Adam answered, suddenly pulling himself away from the view of the gas giant. He grinned sheepishly when he realized that the doctor was smiling at him. "Sorry, I still get caught up in the view sometimes."

"Understandable," Yamamoto said. "I've been here since the station went on line, and I still can't get enough of it. This is the only gas giant I've ever seen that's so close to its primary, and it really does create a remarkable show."

"It sure does," Adam agreed.

"But we do have work to get done," Yamamoto said. "Can you get me current temperature readings for quadrant 17?"

"550 Kelvins," Adam answered, trying his best to focus on the instruments and not the planet itself.

"Harrison's in the orbiter," Yamamoto said. "Can you drop it to 100 kilometers above the cloud tops?"

"Of course," Adam said as he began to manipulate the controls that would drop the small one-man orbiter down towards the clouds. The orbiter had to be controlled from Station Argos because there was always a prisoner on board, since it was dangerous work, and they couldn't let a prisoner operate machinery without a scientist there to observe them. A few prisoners had died in the early years when they'd been allowed to have control, so that had had to change. More recently, there had only been a couple of deaths, and only one of those seemed suspicious.

Adam engaged the solar filter to keep the light from Kepler-11f from interfering with what he was doing. The planet was only a quarter of an astronomical unit away from its star, which made the star loom big and bright any time someone tried looking at it, which was a stupid thing to do, but Adam knew people, and he imagined people looked at the star more often than not.

Even though Limbo was more than twice the diameter of the Earth, it had a fairly low gravity, and Adam sometimes wished he could get down to the surface, if there was a surface, and walk on it. He loved to imagine what the view of the clouds might be like from below.

The pod began to drift as Adam daydreamed again, so he quickly manipulated the controls, hoping Yamamoto hadn't noticed. The doctor took a deep breath, but it wasn't one of alarm or concern, so Adam knew what that meant. "So, how are your roomies getting along?"

There were ten men in the "dorms" where Adam was imprisoned, but he knew what roomies the doctor was talking about. "Lenny's good, Harrington's still a..." He let the words trail off. There was no point in dragging one of the scientists into this. "Harrington is Harrington," he finally said.

Dr. Yamamoto didn't seem satisfied with the answer, but it was the only answer that Adam was prepared to give, and since Yamamoto dropped the conversation, it was pretty obvious that he knew that was all he was going to get out of Adam.

* * *

As Adam approached the dorms, he heard a lot of noise. There was shouting, which sounded like the big voice of Lenny, and other people talking, but he couldn't make anyone's words out. Lenny's were too loud and angry, and everyone else was talking too quietly. He hurried his pace. Something was obviously wrong.

"I'll kill the little weasel," Lenny was shouting as Adam approached. Adam didn't have to try to figure out who Lenny was talking about. He knew. "I swear I'll kill him," Lenny shouted again.

As Adam got closer, he saw blood covering Lenny's face. Whatever had happened was obviously much worse than their usual verbal sparring.

Adam brazenly pushed past several people, including a group of scientists that was trying to figure out what was going on by questioning anyone they could, except Lenny. They seemed to be ignoring him, and for good reason. Adam had never seen him this irate before.

"What happened?" Adam asked as he got closer to Lenny.

"What happened?" Lenny shouted at him. Adam wasn't even sure that Lenny recognized him. "What happened? I'll tell you what happened. That sniveling little weasel dropped something on my face while I was trying to sleep."

Adam scanned the crowd. In between people off to his left, he could occasionally see Harrington's face between the other people's shoulders. The little weasel looked nervous. He normally walked around the dorm and the rest of the station, for that matter, acting like he owned the place, but now he looked scared. It seemed pretty obvious to Adam that Harrington had done something, but he still wasn't sure what.

"Come on," Adam said, grabbing Lenny by the arm and pulling him into the common room. Even though it was a huge breach of protocol, none of the scientists tried to stop them.

"What did he drop on you?" Adam asked.

"I don't know," Lenny answered. "I was sound asleep, and then there was this blinding pain. When I came to, I was covered with blood, but I didn't see anything that he could have done it with."

"Did you see Harrington?"

"No, he was gone, but I have no idea how long I was out of it. He took whatever it was that he hit me with, so I have no idea what it was."

Adam stroked his chin slowly. "Are you sure it was Harrington?"

"Of course," Lenny said, blowing air from his nose. "He's the only one I have a problem with. And if there was anyone else, they wouldn't be cowardly enough to get me in my sleep."

Adam knew Lenny was right, but they had no way of proving it. This would all come down to Lenny's word against Harrington's, and even if Harrington might have been stupid, which he actually wasn't, there wasn't anyone stupid enough to admit to doing what he'd done.

No, they had no way of proving anything.

* * *

Adam wasn't happy about the recent turn of events on Station Argos. Everyone knew that Lenny and Harrington would never get along, but no one, Adam included, had expected it to go this far. But that wasn't what was really bothering Adam about the situation. He was more upset that he was now laying on a couch in a tacky faux-wood coated room talking to Dr. Weinstein.

"So," Dr. Weinstein said, "Why do you think these two don't get along?"

Adam chose to ignore the psychiatrist, instead thinking of what it would be like when the big interstellar ships began coming to the system to refuel on the gasses of Limbo. Some people argued that they shouldn't be allowed to because there were some strange organizations of hydrogen molecules in the atmosphere that the scientists couldn't explain yet. The more passionate ones claimed that it was life of some kind, but until Adam saw proof of that, he'd continue to dream about ships using the planet as a refueling station.

"Mr. Jenkins, I asked you a question," Dr. Weinstein said, and Adam stared blankly at him. "I asked you, why do you think these two don't get along?"

"I don't know," Adam said. "You're the shrink. Why don't you figure it out?"

Of course, Adam actually did know what the problem was, but he wasn't going to give the psychiatrist any easy answers. Instead, he chose to watch the swirling clouds of Limbo through the psychiatrist's window. It was a small window, so Adam could only make out orange clouds, but he could recognize at least a dozen shades of orange in the turbulent eddies.

"Mr. Bishop seems to be implying that Mr. Harrington attacked him," Dr. Weinstein said. "Is this what you believe happened?"

"I was in Observation Pod B with Dr. Yamamoto. How am

I supposed to know what happened?"

"I didn't ask you if Mr. Harrington attacked Mr. Bishop. I asked you if you *thought* that was what happened."

"You got me," Adam said. He could feel his emotions boiling like the clouds of the gas giant. The scientists on broad Argos Station didn't usually bother him, but he'd always had a problem with psychiatrists, and Dr. Weinstein was worse than most. "Harrington's a prick. He might have attacked Lenny. I don't really know, but it wouldn't surprise me."

Dr. Weinstein smiled an odd smile. It wasn't anything like what Adam would have expected for a response. It almost seemed like the shrink was happy with the answers Adam had given, even though that didn't make any sense whatsoever.

* * *

A month passed, and there were no arrests. There weren't even any more interrogations, by security or psychiatrists. It struck Adam as odd, but he let it go. He hadn't wanted to get involved with it from the beginning, and if no one else wanted anything to do with it, then so be it.

Lenny and Harrington were even being more civil than usual. For the first week, Adam had been convinced that Lenny was going to kill Willy, but Lenny's anger quickly subsided, and Adam was glad to see it go.

Adam now found himself in Observation Pod B again. This time Lenny was also there, along with the ever-present Dr. Yamamoto.

Lenny was monitoring the controls closest to the window. The same spot Adam had been in on the day Harrington had attacked Lenny. Adam was standing behind both men monitoring a large storm on the planet that had grown in the last month into the biggest storm they'd seen since Argos Station had been built.

"Harrington's in the orbiter, Mr. Bishop," Dr. Yamamoto said. "Can you drop it to 20 kilometers above the cloud tops? I want to see if we have any hydrogen organization within the storm itself."

"Of course," Lenny answered.

Adam turned and looked at Lenny who had a small smile on his face. It wasn't strange for Lenny to be smiling, but this smile seemed different. *He wouldn't*, Adam thought to himself.

"Dr. Yamamoto," Adam said. "Do you think it might be better if I operate the orbiter? That's pretty close to the surface, and I do have more experience."

"It will be fine," Yamamoto answered.

Adam watched as the small orbiter slowly descended towards the massive storm, a storm that would have consumed all of North America on Earth. The orbiter seemed to bob above the clouds before it suddenly began to plummet.

A scream came over the speakers as Harrington raced towards the top layer of the clouds. Lenny worked frantically at the controls, apparently trying to regain control of the orbiter, but nothing he did seemed to work.

Harrington's scream continued as the small metal orbiter plunged into the towering clouds of the massive storm, but the scream only lasted for a few more seconds. A burst of lightning hit the orbiter as it fell, and then there was silence. Adam watched in horror as the orbiter continued to plummet. Soon they couldn't see it anymore, but the sensors were still reading it. Then it was gone. No more sensor readings. The orbiter had apparently been crushed by the tremendous pressures.

Dr. Yamamoto reached over and touched a button. Then he turned to Lenny. "What happened?"

Lenny was shaking his head. "I don't know. The descent seemed to be going well, but then all of a sudden it was like the signal from us to the orbiter was cut. I couldn't do anything."

Yamamoto turned to Adam. "Did you detect any disruption in the signal?"

Adam looked back and forth between the two men several times. "I ... I don't know. I wasn't really looking for that, so I'm not sure if there was or not."

Two very large men entered Observation Pod B. Both were holding guns, and they both had them aimed at Lenny.

"Mr. Bishop," Yamamoto said. "I'm afraid you're under arrest for the murder of William Harrington."

"What?" Lenny asked. "You've got to be out of your mind."

The two heavily muscled armed men stepped forward and pulled Lenny out of his chair. Lenny was a big man, but they had no problem moving him.

Lenny turned to face Adam, but Adam didn't know what to say. Lenny turned backed to Dr. Yamamoto, but he wasn't saying anything more either. The two men led Lenny from the Pod. Adam didn't know it at the time, but it would be the last time that he'd ever see Lenny.

Adam turned to face Dr. Yamamoto who seemed to have the same smile that Lenny had been wearing earlier.

"That was truly horrible," Dr. Yamamoto said, "But I guess I should have expected it. I suppose I should have listened to you and let you control the descent." He shrugged. "Live and learn, I guess."

"What happens to Lenny now?" Adam asked.

"He's a murderer. He'll go to a penal colony, but I guess it's better than spending an eternity in Limbo like Mr. Harrington."

Dr. Yamamoto stood up and walked past Adam, never even looking at him.

Adam turned and looked at the swirling gas clouds below. Suddenly, Kepler-11f didn't seem as beautiful as it used to.

Kepler-37

The Kepler-37 solar system contains the smallest planet ever discovered outside our solar system. Kepler-37b is the size of our moon. The other two planets in this system are not much bigger; the largest being two times the size of the Earth. These three planets tightly orbit a star about 80% the size of our sun, each circling in 40 days or less, an amazing feat even to Jules Verne. Take three orbiting planetary worlds (or is that two?), some serious but misled scientists, and a good message and you get a romping story of two distinct, but perhaps not dissimilar, worlds.

Kepler-37	Stellar Characteristics
Temperature	5417 Kelvins
Mass	0.8 Solar masses
Radius	0.77 Solar radii
Visual magnitude	10
Distance from Earth	284 Light years

Kepler-37b	Planet Characteristics
Temperature	650 Kelvins
Mass	<2 Earth masses
Radius	0.30 Earth radii
Orbital Period	13.4 days
Distance from Star	0.10 AUs

Continued on next page.

Kepler-37c	Planet Characteristics
Temperature	560 Kelvins
Mass	<2 Earth masses
Radius	0.74 Earth radii
Orbital Period	21.3 days
Distance from Star	0.74 AUs

Kepler-37d	Planet Characteristics
Temperature	450 Kelvins
Mass	<2 Earth masses
Radius	2.1 Earth radii
Orbital Period	39.9 days
Distance from Star	0.21 AUs

A Mango and Two Peanuts
Steve B. Howell

"Hey! Grab that bolt before it flies off into the void and hits the bubble!"

"Got it Krau," Oaak yelled into his helmet microphone. "Sorry, just getting tired. This space work always strains my muscles. These damn suits have no flexibility! Why are we fixing this old blocking screen anyway? Are they planning to reuse it after all this time?"

"Well," called Krau, "some folks at the Center got new payment credits to continue their long-term communication experiment. Not that I care, but this work will keep my company in business until my daughter takes over. It might even pay for her retirement!"

"That's fine for you, Krau," mumbled Oaak, "but what about me? I don't want to work on old thermal wind sails my whole life. Fix this motor, add another energy thruster, increase orbital speed, now decrease speed ... not what I call fun. Give me a turbo-boost two-seat thermal thruster and let me cruise the system." He imagined himself blasting from one planet to another with the throttle wide open.

Oaak missed the holder and another bolt flew off. This time it hit Krau's helmet and veered off.

"Damn it, Oaak!" Krau shouted into his helmet mike. "Now I have to unharness and chase down that bolt. Will you pay attention?"

Oaak was not even listening—a green and purple two-seat thermal thruster was burned into his brain. "What? Oh sorry," he said ... but he was not.

"Krau, this is Org, why are you unhooking?"

"Org, another bolt broke off. It's drifting away. I need to chase it down. Oaak will finish the thermal testing and start up the sail, over." Krau thumbed the intercom to the internal net. "Oaak, I'm tired of covering for you! Get those thermal tests done and start up the sail, now!"

"Yeah, okay," droned Oaak. "I'll have that done in a jiffy ... almost there ... There got it!"

"Org," called Oaak, "all done. Tests are one hundred percent. The sail is running on auto. Orbit period set to 3044 units,
up three percent from yesterday."

* * *

"We need more memory! The photometric information
won't turn into light curves by itself you know. I have to have
these data all analyzed and delivered to the archive data server
by next Friday. Will you hurry up?"

"Man, I just don't get this process. How do you expect
me to understand any of your blabber?" Jared held his hands
out to his sides. "I was hired to provide quality control of the
time series data, not to be your computer fix-it guy. I'll go get
Marko."

Hundreds of graphs appeared on the screens that covered
most of the room's video wall. Each looked nearly the same—a
wiggly line that dropped in a flat-bottomed U-shape for a
while, then recovered to its higher normal level again. Each of
the graphs represented a possible alien planet—an exoplanet—
which Dave and many others were analyzing in an attempt to
find which ones were real.

"Look at them!" cried Dave waving his arms at the graphs,
"look at all the new ones. There are dozens of them, many with
more than one planet orbiting. I want them all catalogued."
Dave pointed to Marko. "Give me the list of the multis as soon
as you're done."

"I can't do that, Dave...", Marko muttered under his breath,
as he started to record the data in a spreadsheet.

Jared folded his arms and turned to Marko. "So, what's the
deal with all these graphs? Can you explain them to me? Dave
is always going on about them with great enthusiasm, but, to
me, the graphs all look like lines with a break in the middle."

"Sure thing, it's actually quite easy. That's why Dave can
understand it!" Marko winked. "You see, the telescope out in
space stares at a lot of stars. It watches them day and night—
being in space and all—and waits for a planet orbiting the alien
sun to move directly in front." He picked up a couple of tennis
balls from the desk and moved one around the other. When
the orbiting ball was between the "sun" and Jared, he continued. "This is called a transit. When we look at the graphs, we

see the change in the brightness of the star as time passes. The U-shaped drop in light happens when the exoplanet passes in front." Marko began juggling the balls as he continued. "Now for the simple part, for a certain size star, the larger the drop in brightness, the larger the planet. Multis, as Dave called them, are alien solar systems. Systems of multiple worlds orbiting other suns. Our solar system has nine planets ... well eight I guess if you buy into that Pluto-is-a-dwarf-planet thing. I mean, c'mon it has five moons!" He shrugged. "Anyway, solar systems with many planets—in particular, many small, perhaps rocky planets, are seemingly common. These multiple planet systems are what Dave likes to study in detail." Marko caught the balls and dropped them back on the desk.

Over in the corner, Dave stared intently at forty-two graphs on the video wall. Kepler-37, a fairly normal looking G7 main sequence star, a star much like the sun, kept drawing his interest. Kepler-37 is similar in age to our sun but about 400 degrees cooler, slightly smaller—0.7 times the radius—and less massive. This star caught Dave's interest as he noticed that it had three planets orbiting it. The innermost planet candidate was the smallest exoplanet yet discovered, just slightly larger than the Earth's moon. The middle and outer planets were just a bit smaller than the Earth, a size which meant that they had a surface gravity capable of holding onto water and an atmosphere, as well as being likely to have a rocky surface.

His eyes were glued to the computer screens and he kept spouting information into the air as the plots flashed by. "Orbital periods are less than forty days. Wow! That is short .... Middle planet is smaller than the third one .... The alien sun seems to have starspots just like our sun...." and so on for another half hour or so.

"Hey Jared," called Dave, "come look at this multi, there is something strange going on with one of the planet transits. It doesn't really have the correct shape on the graph for a planet." He pointed to a plot labeled Kepler-37b.

Jared studied the plot for a few moments, then looked at Dave and said, "Huh? That *is* odd."

"It doesn't seem to fit as well as the other two planets orbiting Kepler-37", Dave mused over this for a bit and shook his head. "Maybe I used the wrong parameters for the host star radius or something. Let me check."

Finally, the plots stopped flashing on the video screens. The analysis was finished for the time being. The computers had produced another round of information to be mulled over in the coming weeks. Dave and Jared stared at a batch of print-outs.

Marko looked over their shoulders. "Anyone hungry?"

* * *

Duba had just started working at the Center a few orbits ago and was a bit nervous being alone at the controls. She had worked on control systems when in school, but this was larger and more complex than anything she had ever seen. Duba was setting the speed control monitor for the sail when she noticed a small crumpled note lying near the ON button. On the note was scribbled, *a mango and two peanuts.* It made no sense. What was a mango?

Dar Bradbury walked in just then and Duba asked her about the note. "Oh that note? I was trying it out a few days ago, but with the speed control broken I decided to wait," Dar mumbled, staring at the daily record charts.

"What are you talking about?" Duba asked.

"Ah! The use of the sails, our great experiment," quipped Dar. "We recently started a new communication program using Sail 17. This is why we hired you and started upgrading the sail. Do you know the connection between the sail operations and our work here at the Center?" As Duba slightly shook her head no, Dar said, "Come with me." They both walked out the door, across the hall, and entered the lab.

The lab was divided into two parts. One part held a set of computers used for coding the words along with their operators. On the other side was a long row of desks with work stations on them. The desks were well organized by function, size, and shape. At each desk, lab-coated interns sat on one side with a recording device in hand and beings from a variety of worlds sat across from them. The interns held up cards with words or symbols on them, waited a few seconds and typed something into their recording device.

"So," said Dar, "what do you think? Pretty simple huh?"

"Well, I guess so," Duba replied a bit perplexed. Duba did not want to seem as if she was completely unaware of what the company she worked for did. After all she had told them at her interview that she knew all about the Center for Creative Thinking. Of course, what she did not know were the internal details. These were not generally made available outside the Center. Now here, in front of her boss, she did not want to seem ignorant, but in fact seeing a room full of aliens was a bit disconcerting. "Ah, can you tell me why all these aliens are here?"

Dar looked at Duba with a slight frown on all three of her lips. "The Center operates a number of ultralight ships for the purpose of scientific discovery. Our recruitment branch robots go aboard these ships to gather up volunteers from the alien worlds we discover. We stopped our older procedures of making them come along. From these beings we learn their language and about their worlds, what their struggles are, and what is likely to be the best communication method to use."

"Ah, I see," said Duba, even though she didn't.

"Duba, notice how the Fruids always turn their heads when they smile and how the legs of the Bappo curl under when they laugh."

Duba watched as an intern stood up from a desk and said goodbye to a blue, smooth looking creature, which she thought must be an XX-Gondo. She had only seen pictures of this type of being but never had seen one in real life.

The intern gave the recording device to one of the computer operators. "Wow, that'll be a fun one to code. It'll really test the speed control on the sails." The operator stood akimbo and tried to make his voice echo as he said: "We will soon know how well those new thermal thrusters react!"

Dar reminded Duba that she needed to get back to her station and make sure the speed control on Sail 17 was working properly. "I want a print out of the speed changes for 17 by the end of the code sequence. Try to make sure they occur quickly this time. Each change needs to be less than one-tenth of the orbital period."

Upon returning to her lab, Duba fell into a dreamy state and began to think of how fun it was to slide down the metallic hills outside on a Wolfram sled. As a girl, she used to be very good at sledding, only slipping her feet off into the molten surface layer once or twice. Her metal-coated boots heated quickly, but her fast reactions brought her feet back onto the sled—she didn't even burn a single toe. She always had a bent for technology, even as a child, and now had a job where she could apply it. Somehow she would figure out how the alien beings in the lab were connected to her operating a large thermal sail.

Snapping back to reality and Sail 17, Duba noticed a note attached to her console. *Make sure to set the speed control to the 3:1 level at least once every 10 orbits.* What did that mean? The 3:1 level? Dar was sitting a few tables away and Duba decided to ask her what the note meant. She was never going to fully appreciate her work and its importance if she did not understand it. "Dar," she said, "did you leave me this note? The one about the 3:1 level?"

Dar turned to her and said, "Oh you mean the 3-to-1 resonance compliance we need to make sure to do?" Duba looked puzzled and Dar immediately picked up on it. "How well did you do in your celestial mechanics class? Remember resonance driving? The Driver?

"Oh, the sails' main energy source. I get it. We get the power to keep the sails in orbit by using the planet tri-LUK. The outer planet has an orbital period about three times that of the sails and if we keep the sails in a near resonance orbit, we can use tri-LUK's orbital energy as a gravitational boost to pump the sails along. The solar-powered thrusters then simply need to make small adjustments to the orbit to allow for the required speed ups and slow downs." Duba was breathless after this fast soliloquy, but felt very proud. Her study of orbital mechanics had paid off.

* * *

"I just don't get it," Dave said, showing the plots to Dr. Morbius. "The two outer planets show a perfect alignment in the time of their transits but the inner planets' transit seems to speed up and slow down from time to time. At first I thought it was an effect of general relativity, you know like the orbit of Mercury in our solar system. But when I calculate the terms out, the effect we observe is far too large."

"Well, well," droned Morbius in a near whisper, "maybe the answer lies in the signal."

"Huh!" Dave frowned a bit disheartened. "What does that mean?"

"Well, you know that you are observing a phenomenon, you know it changes, and you believe the changes are real. Therefore, you must use the force, Luke." Morbius let out a giggle and Dave rolled his eyes. "You must take the variations at their face value and look into what they tell you. Do they vary in a regular pattern? Do they vary randomly? These are the things you must now turn your attention to." And with that final word, Dr. Morbius turned on his heels and walked out of the room.

As usual, Dave was baffled by the comments. He blinked at the video screens but remained in a state of confusion, a typical reaction when Dr. Morbius gave him advice. Yet comments from Morbius, albeit odd, always seemed to be highly pertinent in the end. They always seemed to lead in interesting directions. So, what could the variations in the transit times mean? Dave didn't know but he was going to find out.

* * *

Oaak stuffed the plag and vitor sandwich into his mouth, just as the auto-helmet mechanism clicked closed. He could not talk to give the okay to seal the helmet, and the outside doors were beginning to open.

"Damn it, Oaak," shouted Krau as he whacked down on Oaak's helmet to set the seal just as the doors opened to free space.

"UUHMmmmnuuu." Oaak's words were garbled as he tried to finish chewing the sandwich, tossing his head back in an attempt to swallow.

"We have to get those thermal thrusters tuned today for sure," Krau said sternly. "The alignment must be perfect by one-half an orbit from now. The Driver is lining up." Planet tri-LUK was nearing its aphelion position and soon would be able to provide its maximum boost to Sail 17, the one currently not functioning at spec. Krau's reputation was on the line. He wanted to perform well as a part of this large project. Dr. Dar Bradbury's new project was going to mean a long contract for his company. She told him that they were going to phase 3 communications with a small planet only 284 light years away. She was very excited given that this alien world was so close. "A weekend trip," was her comment.

"It took the planet forever to finally develop the necessary technology," Dr. Bradbury had told him. "Most societies begin looking for other worlds far sooner, and by looking, they almost always develop very sensitive telescopes. We are all so visual." Thus, Sail 17 was now all-important. Krau could not let her down.

"Oaak, are you ready? Start the thermal thrusters. Set them at positive friction and speed range three."

"Started and set, working perfectly," Oaak boomed with authority. "Told you it would."

Krau had to agree. The thrusters took control of the sail and he noted right away its positive momentum drive was on and operating exactly as planned. Very soon now, the sail would start its planned sequence of speeding up for a number of orbits and then slowing down for some. The sail would continue in this pre-programmed complex pattern, firing its thrusters under computer control when needed, hopefully performing as planned. This was a thing of beauty, an object nearly one-third the size of their home planet, orbiting their sun every thirteen days, more or less, and powered only by gravity from tri-LUK with a little help from some small sun-powered thrusters.

* * *

"Let's review the data." Dave sat with his group staring at piles of plots in front of them on the floor. "If I take the exact time when the transit of the middle planet, Kepler-37c, happens and plot it for each transit, they all line up perfectly. That means its orbital period, as expected, is exactly the same each time it goes around its sun. If I do the same for Kepler-37d, the third and outermost planet, they line up as well. But when I plot this up for Kepler-37b, the small inner planet, they are all over the place. They seem to occur earlier than expected at times and later at other times. Every now and then, they occur exactly when expected."

"Let me see your plot," said Toma, a young postdoc working in the group. "I once read this book by some old science guy—Segan or Sagan or something like that. In it he mentioned that humans placed messages on gold records in a sort of code. The records were then launched on spacecraft in hopes that someday an alien race would find the records and decode the information. I think the coded messages said things like, *Take me to your leader."*

At this, they all laughed and starting talking about old movies they had seen. The conversation gave way to quoting old sci-fi movie lines. "Klaatu barada nikto." "Watch the Skies."

"Hey, wait a minute," strained Toma's small voice, "I think I see something here. The patterns of the transit times might be a code. If the data is divided by the orbital period and then placed in a time sequence..." Feeling there was nothing to lose, Toma typed a few keystrokes on Dave's laptop and voila, the manipulated data appeared. They all looked stunned, a clear pattern had emerged—the apparent random times of the transits of the smallest exoplanet ever discovered were not random at all. The times fell into a number of well defined sets and these were laid out before them in what looked like a regular pattern—a code. The group had found a coded message, a coded alien message.

* * *

Ding. Ding. Ding! Ding!

"Huh," snorted Duba as she shook her head waking from an unplanned nap. The coaster alarm was ringing so loudly, she hoped no one else heard it. The alarm had sounded to allow the operator a chance to override or stop the mechanism. Hitting the silence button, Duba typed in the sequence of commands, stopping the alarm and releasing the coaster brakes on Sail 17. This was a typical start-up item she needed to do but it had slipped her mind. She had been wading through a number of technical manuals, trying to find the reason for the recruited aliens. Duba had fallen behind in the sail tests she was required to do each time any new maintenance work was performed. Unbenownst to Duba, an automatic report of this delay in the tests would be sent to her section head. This would be the first such report Duba had since starting work at the Center.

The sail indicators whirled into action, all green and

working properly. "Whew, that was close," Duba hissed. "Maybe I caught it in time." Sitting down again at the technical reports and breathing more normally, Duba looked across the hall and noticed that the interns in the lab were all huddled around a console yammering loudly. Checking the lights again—all green—she decided to see what was happening in the lab.

As she approached the crowd, the talk became loud enough for her pick out specific words and phrases. "...and then I showed him number X35..." and "...never saw a puddle that large..." The interns were laughing loudly. None of this made any sense to Duba. She realized that she had no idea what happened in this part of the Center, how her Sail 17 work was related to it, and why this place was given such a high status in their society. Well, now was as good a time as ever to find out.

She moved into the crowd and walked up to a young intern in a purple lab coat with a large plastic flower in his lapel. "Hey," she said. "What's all the fuss, I mean, what are you guys doing here?"

The intern turned to her. "We just received our long-term report from the Alpha Centauri monitoring group and we're a big success, larger then we imagined, a rating of 9JS. That is like off the charts!"

"Oh, Oh my!" Duba exclaimed. "Congratulations." She turned and started to walk away, more confused now than ever.

"Don't go," said the intern. "We're all going to the conference room to celebrate. Want to come along?" He was smiling so nice and Duba was sure that her sail was working properly. She decided to go along.

At the end of the large table in the middle of the room sat a tall, pyramid-shaped glass item, etched with the words, *To the Alpha Centauri CCT Team, best wishes and hearty chuckles for their 9JS award from MG 10087A.* Sitting beside the award, was a large electronic box with blinking lights and a few dials.

Duba looked at the box and then at the purple-coated intern who blurted, "How do you like it? I helped create it. It's why we won the award."

"Oh, I like it very much," Duba smiled. "That box helped

you win the award?"

"Indeed!" he beamed proudly. "It contains a large selectory from all the beings we have interviewed, all alphabetically arranged by personality. It took many orbits to put the memory cells together but it will become the standard in our work and soon will be applied to all our projects."

Duba was eager to hear more but was afraid she'd get lost in the details if she pursued the topic further. "I was hired to run Sail 17," she said shyly, rocking back and forth a bit. "I'm a controls technician."

"Oh, Sail 17 is very important to the new project Dr. Bradbury is working on."

"Really?"

"What? Don't they tell you anything over there?"

"Not much I guess. Well I mean I just started working here at the Center. They just give us our orders and don't really tell us much about how we fit into the big picture."

"That's a shame. The important part is to know that you're doing your part to allow our research groups to design and send light patterns. Patterns which convey the messages our society feels are so important."

* * *

Running into the room, Toma shouted, "Got it! That old library is useful for something." She turned to the index and then to a story near the middle of the volume she held in her hands. "Here it is, 'The Gold-Bug', one of the first true detective stories and in it, a universal method to start any decoding process. Single symbols are most likely to be words such as *a* or *I*, while repeated sequences are likely to be longer words with the symbols being the letters in order of their most common occurrence, e, then a, then o, and so on."

"Where do you get this stuff?" Jared said, feeling a smile coming on as he looked at Toma's face, "You are really odd, but ... cool!"

Dave looked perplexed and made a suspicious snort. "Are you kidding? We get some coded message from outer space and you think we can translate it using a 19th century story?"

"Well, I don't know," Toma uttered, not looking up while working feverishly on her laptop. "You got any better ideas?"

Using the last few months of data for Kepler-37b, the small inner exoplanet candidate, Toma began to match her "Gold-Bug" ideas to the patterns she found in the transits. The pattern in their measured times, some arriving too early and some too late, seemed to indicate that the object was not a real exoplanet. It was some sort of variable source used to send coded messages. The others began to get drawn in as well, not from any belief that this decoding made any sense but they were carried by the feeling of the moment that it just might work. They might be the first ones to decode a message from the stars. A message that might contain the key to the beginning of the Universe or plans to a faster-than-light spaceship. Whatever it was, they were drawn in.

Hours passed as computer programs were written, translation ideas failed and were reborn. Some of the group just sat in the corner and read "The Gold-Bug" for inspiration.

Finally, after a third pot of coffee and at least two stale sandwiches, Toma yelled, "I got it! Well I got some of it anyway." On her computer screen a graph appeared. On the top, the graph showed the regular patterns found in the data collected, the times coming too early or too late. Underneath, a few translated words appeared: *Man, Wife and ... Elephant.*

* * *

Dar entered the lab conference room and saw Duba standing near the obelisk talking to the purple-coated man. "Ah, there you are," she said. " I've been looking for you. I see that you are not drenched. Dero here usually spares no one from his *flower power.*"

"I guess I was too excited by the award to think of that now," Dero said feeling the eyes of Dar burning him.

"Well, then, may Duba return to her work? I'm sure you realize the importance of our messaging today. We are moving Sail 17 into pattern 23-4Z for the first time and we want to get it right. There is nothing as bad as sending out the wrong language to a planet and then waiting for eons for them to catch up." Dar moved in between Dero and Duba and slowly walked her back across the hall and into the sail control room.

"You know, Duba," Dar said quietly, "our ancients felt very strongly about the messages we send out. They are very important and they do help societies learn to get along. The messages teach them what is important and how to live their lives. The messages help them realize that some things are very important to study and to believe in."

"Well, that sounds very important." Duba turned red.

"Our ancients started sending messages out many generations ago as they were inspired to teach others of their beliefs. At first, they tried actual visitations, but mainly found that the aliens got scared and hostile. Sometimes, the aliens even started blaming others of their same species for the visits. Center studies have since shown that it takes time for the immature worlds to accept and benefit from such directness.

Duba was engrossed in the story now. "So, we don't visit anyone anymore?"

"Well, once the other worlds are ready, we establish direct communication. It appears that Alpha Centauri may be close to that stage. We did try to send our messages in a more direct way once, using clones. Have you seen the clone lab? Remember the early ruckus here at this station when the controversy occurred about cloning us as well as cloning aliens?"

"Sure, I remember that," Duba perked up. "I was a kid and my mother told me about the experiments. I never knew we used clones for anything to do with alien worlds."

"Yes, we tried the clones as a medium of direct communication, sending them off to alien worlds, using shapes and forms that we thought would fit in—sometimes cloning the recruits themselves, hoping they might be accepted. Their job was to spread our message into their society. However, we found out from our monitoring groups that this only worked well in small groups and in some sub-species, but the messages were not accepted as a whole as we had hoped."

Duba was on the edge of her seat, "What happened then?"

"Our light communication project and the communication laboratory was formed and the rest, as they say, is history."

"Ah ha," Duba said, while thinking *huh?*

"Our society has greatly benefited from the messages we seek to share. We live in peace and harmony with many other worlds because of them. I hope you realize that and can understand why your job is so important. I received a notice today about your delay in the start-up testing of Sail 17. Such reports can cause you to lose your job. But, the messages we send out inspire me as well." Dar turned and walked to the door, but stopped before leaving, "Duba, one more delay, and messages or not, you are gone."

* * *

Silence filled the room. No one could speak. They all just stared at the screen. Each in turn began to realize what, and perhaps where, these coded messages came from. Was the answer to life on Earth or Creation itself contained within the set of coded transit observations they had collected? Their work had just begun.

Dave had been skeptical at first, and maybe even at second. He could not believe it'd be so easy. He would be famous. Humanity awaited his translations of the alien messages. His life would be set. Fame and fortune were his.

Toma's programs had been working on the coded messages night and day. During that time, Dave had been showing up now and then to 'point out her mistakes' and to prod her along. He kept saying he'd like to help, but that he has been busy putting together the press release for later that week. Getting the wording just right and such, so that he and of course all of them, would get the proper credit for this momentous discovery. Who should be there when they made the announcement? World leaders? Religious leaders? Famous scientists? ... Movie Stars? He was not sure.

* * *

The literature about the Center that Duba received when she was hired was still lying on the shelf underneath her work bench. Sail 17 was in full action, working perfectly. She noted too, that many other sails, all controlled by similar technicians, were doing their things as well. Over fifty sails in all were controlled from within this room. All orbited close to their parent star, choreographed to perfection to send *the message* out to many alien worlds. But why?

Technical brochure S-23-A seemed to have the answer. After trying actual contact—real visits to try to meet other species face-to-face—and after sending clones to live and work among the species and spread the word, the ancients discovered something almost universally true about alien societies. They are prone to fear and mistrust when under stress. Additionally, the ancients learned that single beings can only influence a few. Sometimes they influenced more, but only for a limited time period. But if a majority of the species found a common goal or belief to work on together, the result could be powerful. It could provide an influence for many of the beings that lasted for a very long time. Communicating to a sentient species from afar, from an apparently superior being—a mysterious source that they could never quite fully understand—could provide such an influence. This sort of messaging provided a deeper meaning to them and their entire society, one accepted and believed in. They responded to the message and their common acceptance of it.

This was the principle behind the correct operation of the sails. They were the prime communication method used by Duba's world to send out the messages, the source of so much hope to create better societies on worlds throughout the galaxy. And, when each species in turn was ready, allowed direct communication between worlds.

Duba sat down and let out a deep breath, "Wow, my role is really important."

* * *

Toma walked into Dave's office. She had finally translated all she could given the time constraints, the data they had in hand, and Dave's pushing to notify the world as quickly as possible. Toma had turned the graphs into test strings, each one being a partial translation of the full set of the patterns received. Each pattern was then matched and cross-referenced to each other set and the "Gold-Bug" method applied. She showed the translations to Dave.

His smile got larger as his eyes widened. "Are you sure about this?"

Toma laughed. "I am."

Dave sat back in his chair and called someone on the phone. "Hey, we're going to need some different people lined up for the press event. I'm not sure right now but I'll be in touch." He hung up the phone and dropped the papers on his desk. He started to laugh.

The translations were only partial, but their meaning was

clear. They were indeed messages to better humankind and create a peaceful society. The translated words read:

A man walks into a bar...

My wife, please...

Knock, Knock...

Elephant in pajamas...

priest, a rabbi, and...

...A mango and two peanuts...

Kepler-16

Kepler-16 was the first circumbinary planet ever discovered, that is a planet that orbits a binary star. In this close binary star, components A & B are both smaller and cooler then our sun and are orbited at some distance by a Saturn-like planet. At only 200 light years away from Earth, this binary star and its attendant planet are one of the closest Kepler planet systems to be discovered. Turn on the lights, lock the doors, and get a buddy for this one. This story will assure you of the fact that space travel can really go to the dogs.

Kepler-16 A,B	Stellar Characteristics
Temperature	4450 / 2800 Kelvins
Mass	0.68 / 0.2 Solar masses
Radius	0.64 / 0.2 Solar radii
Visual magnitude	12
Distance from Earth	199 Light years
Orbital Period	41 days

Kepler-16b	Planet Characteristics
Temperature	185 Kelvins
Mass	106 Earth masses
Radius	8.5 Earth radii
Orbital Period	229 days
Distance from Star	0.7 AUs

The Company You Keep
M. H. Bonham

Wolf wasn't sure what to think when we saw the alien. The ridge of hair on his back rose from his shoulders down to the base of his tail, frosty and red-silver in the twin suns' ruddy light. Despite the twin suns, the sky was a deep blue, mirroring the rolling landscape of bluish-white snow, ice, and odd crystalline "trees" that stretched their branches and translucent needles to catch what little sunlight they could.

We had seen something like it before—a few ridges back—but this animal had pincers and looked more ferocious. It chattered and clacked its pincers, its ten beautifully translucent blue legs skittering on the bluish snow like ice picks.

"Easy, boy," I said, my teeth chattering, despite the heat suit. I would reach out to grab the dog by his collar if my hands stopped shaking for a moment. They alternated between numb and clammy like some goddamn chicken thawing in the refrigerator. Wolf didn't mind the cold, but his ancestors came from the Arctic, while mine evolved from Africa, and didn't have enough sense to stay where it was warm.

Wolf looked up curiously, his expressive brown eyes beneath two white dots. His markings gave him a mask-like appearance, and he wagged his bushy tail before turning again to the life form. Wolf really wasn't a wolf, although I called him that. His real name wasn't Wolf either, but he answered to it a lot better than the name NASA had given him. Wolf was an Alaskan Malamute, too tall and lean to be show quality. Some brass in the upper echelons had thought bringing dogs on space exploration was a good idea, and despite the protests, they got their way.

Wolf sniffed again and then turned and lifted his leg, pissing on the pristine ice. I groaned, but didn't really feel upset. The dog wasn't polluting any more than the humans did and the composition of the permafrost would absorb the urine nicely. Once colonist craft started coming in, we wouldn't worry much about a little dog piss.

The thing chattered again. Wolf's expression turned

mischievous and he batted at the critter with his forepaw.

"Stop it," I said crossly. "We don't know if it's venomous or not."

Wolf didn't seem to hear, despite those lovely triangular ears. He bounded after the alien and nosed it. The critter whirled around and clacked its pincers at Wolf. He leapt back, still head down, ears pricked forward, and nose pointing at the crab-like thing. I pulled out a collection tool and bag and gently caught the alien between the tool's four grasping arms and deposited it in the bag. Wolf trotted up to me, obviously pleased with himself.

"You could've gotten bit." I didn't bother to comment on his goofy expression as I tagged the bag. What in the hell was I going to call this? A Kepler ice crab? I'd have to make up some ostentatious Latin name for the thing, but an ice crab suited it well enough. Not that I thought it was in any way related to crustaceans back home.

I looked upward into the darkening sky. Kepler-16b glowed above us like a stormy jewel, so reminiscent of Saturn, despite the lack of rings and the twin suns' ruddy glow. It was getting late and we'd be passing along the dark side of the planet soon enough. That would bring more than just a chill to the air.

I began to turn when a low rumble and a telltale whine interrupted my thoughts. A passenger shuttle from one of the transit ships streaked across the sky and turned to make its final approach. Wolf and I watched for a long moment as the autopilot kicked the ship into the right path. The lenticular clouds to the west combined with high cirrus suggested a ripping wind.

"Shouldn't have planted the base so close to the ice volcanoes," I muttered. Landon, our head geologist, was still trying to decide if the moon had plate tectonics. Oh, it was seismically active, all right. The lava tubes and hot geysers we used for heat and water were proof enough, but whether true tectonics was going on was an ongoing study.

Wolf trotted beside me as I walked toward the lab. I needed to drop off the ice crab before it died so we could study it. We had already found some interesting animals that browsed the ice needle trees. One was a large eight-legged herbivore with a shaggy down-like coat that startled easily. They tended to graze at night in the coldest, darkest times making me wonder what hunted them. Wolf had gone crazy chasing them the first time we saw them but broke off when they charged him, heads lowered with four horns on their heads and sharp spine ridges that served as armor. I now kept him on an electronic leash that I could turn on if he strayed too far or went after some of the fauna.

It had been a quiet afternoon, but that had more to do with the fact I shut my comm off. It was my day off, dammit, even if I felt like collecting specimens with Wolf. The last time I kept my comm link on, Harry had called me in for some stupid something or other.

The passenger ship waggled a bit before touching down at the airport. I frowned. There wasn't supposed to be a landing for at least a week, if I remember the schedule. Reluctantly, I flicked on my comm, expecting for the worst.

Nothing on my personal band. Good. I tapped the scan to pick up the airport tower and got the usual chatter. Nothing out of the ordinary. I sighed with relief. "Dodged that bullet, huh?" I said to Wolf. He just wagged his tail.

* * *

Kepler-16b moonbase isn't impressive. In fact, the Antarctic bases have more room than we do when it comes to square feet. The preassembled units look a bit like a trailer park connected together in a series of tubes. Space costs money out here especially when being shipped back and forth via a warp bubble. The bigger you warp space, the faster you need something, the more energy you need. I don't even want to think about what it cost to get Wolf and me here.

Wolf and I were walking through the hatch to get back to our quarters when Wolf turned and gave a quick yip in greeting. Damn.

"Marshall, where in the hell have you been?"

I turned around and brandished the specimen bag, hoping to distract Harry. "Hey, I found another life form. Need to get it into stasis before it dies."

Harry's face turned red and he squinted at me. He's a hard-ass, to be sure, but my easy smile sometimes throws him off guard. "Cinthia..." he rumbled.

Wolf echoed his words with a deep grumble of his own. "Easy, big fella," I said, running my fingers through the Malamute's neck fur while meeting Harry's gaze. About forty and fit as they came for a station commander, a shock of white hair around the temples broke up his dark brown curls. He wore one of those ubiquitous NASA jumpsuits that we all had. His fit better than mine did, which isn't saying much. Right then my heat suit worked overtime and sweat dripped down my face. Why couldn't it work this good outside?

"Why didn't you have your comm on?" Harry eyed the big dog nervously. I don't think he likes them.

"It's my day off."

"And you decided for some extracurricular exploration?"

"I signed out."

"Damn it, Cinthia, you know damn well you're supposed to have your comm link on. I don't give a flying rat's backside that you got some sort of prize for discovering whatever you did back on Earth..."

"It was a Nobel Prize for identifying the first alien life form," I said wearily. "And it was a fluke. We were a team and it just so happened to be me..."

"Then behave like we're a team. I expect my head Xenobiologist to act better. It's dangerous out there..."

"What's got a burr up your butt?" I snapped. "Wolf was with me, and the only thing we've seen other than those icicle trees are horned beasts, bacteria, and ice crabs."

"Kevin's missing."

"Huh?" That stopped me cold. "Seriously?"

"Yeah, he hasn't called in."

I frowned. Kevin was my junior partner. He's kind of green when it comes to space exploration, but he's a good kid. A little moonstruck when he met me, I guess he learned about my discoveries in college a couple of years ago. "He should've been over near the western ridge."

"We found his buggy. It was trashed."

"Trashed?" I blinked. "He have a wreck?"

"No, trashed. Like something attacked it."

My mouth went dry. "We've got to find him—send out a search party. We must find him..." Wolf sidled up to me and pressed his big head in my hands.

"I've already got the drones searching for him using infrared signatures."

"But the horned beasts will throw it off. And who knows what's out there."

"I've assembled search parties already. Command has been notified Earth-side. They've sent someone here."

I blinked. "Here? Already?"

Harry nodded. "Get cleaned up—it's brass. When you're ready, I need you to take a look at the buggy and tell me what ripped it apart."

* * *

I had just finished a shower and gotten dressed when the intercom sounded. "Doctor Marshall? Lieutenant Anderson is waiting for you."

Wolf had lifted his head and pricked his ears at the voice running through our tiny room that served as an office, bedroom, and kitchen. He was lying on the bed to avoid being underfoot—I didn't blame him for that, so I didn't scold him. I was one of the lucky ones with a real shower and toilet; most people on the base didn't have the luxury and had to use the communal showers and bathrooms. I had hung the damp heat suit on the door and rummaged through my all-too-small closet for shoes instead of slippers.

"Who the hell is Lieutenant Anderson?" I replied, feeling a bit testy. The only thing more irritating than having someone interrupt you after taking a shower is to interrupt you while you're in the shower.

"He came in today, Earth-side."

"Directly?"

"Yes, Ma'am."

I glanced at the clock. Four forty-five already. "Okay, tell him I'll meet him at 1700." I clicked the intercom off and whistled. Wolf looked up curiously. "That's huge, Wolf," I said softly. "They don't burn that kind of energy for space tours."

I began to fret a bit. We're almost two hundred light years away, and while a warp bubble can travel at whatever you'd like, it requires a lot of energy. I couldn't believe that he had just come for Kevin's disappearance. Harry had sent a quantum-entangled message about it, but why the Earthers cared was beyond me. Don't get me wrong. Kevin's a good kid, if inexperienced, but he never struck me as having ties to anyone big. He wasn't necessarily the brightest bulb in the pack, but he was competent enough to work for me.

"Come on, Wolf. Let's see what the lieutenant wants."

* * *

Lieutenant Jack Anderson could be a recruiting poster-boy for the Marines. Clean cut, clean shaven, uniform beyond crisp, he made me feel sloppy. My own hair, mousy-brown and tied back had enough gray to tell him I could be his mother. Years of sitting at a computer and a microscope had taken the edge off my muscles and the lieutenant's presence reminded me I needed to hit the gym again.

Wolf followed me like a shadow. Normally he's mister puppy charm, but something about the lieutenant kept him at bay. I trusted Wolf's judgment, but I decided to make a good impression before I told the brass to get lost.

Harry fidgeted as I entered. No doubt he wanted me to behave.

"Welcome to Tatooine, Lieutenant," I said, offering my hand. "I'm Doctor Cinthia Marshall."

Harry groaned and rolled his eyes, but Anderson had a quizzical expression. "Tatooine?"

"Actually, it's more like the ice planet, Hoth, than Tatooine, but the binary makes some pretty spectacular sunsets." I paused. "You ever watch *Star Wars?*"

"No." Anderson looked down at my hand as if I were offering him an ice crab instead of a friendly gesture. He glanced at Wolf. "Is that Laika?"

I winced. "He goes by Wolf." I didn't want to get into the story why I really didn't want to call him "Laika," which incidentally means "dog" in Russian. Yes, he was named after the first dog in space. But Laika was a female, and sadly ended up getting burned up in reentry. I had no desire for a repeat.

"That's not his name," Anderson said.

"No, well, you can call him Laika, but he won't listen to you."

Anderson ignored my answer and turned to Harry. "What

have the drones found?"

Harry shook his head. "Just the horned beasts. We found some footprints in the snow near the buggy..."

"You didn't tell me that," I snapped.

"I didn't think I was reporting to you." Harry glared. "In fact, I believe it's the other way around, *Doctor*."

My face grew hot. *Asshole.* "Life forms are my department," I said. "It would've been helpful, *Commander*, if you had told me about them. I've been looking for a top-tier predator since we've come to this moon."

"Looks like we found one." Anderson interrupted me.

"Maybe." I felt testy. I didn't need some smartass, Earth-side lieutenant telling me my job either.

Harry ignored my comment. "I'll show you both the footage from the wreck. I'll need Laika to scout around and see if he can track them."

"What can that mutt do?" Anderson asked.

"He's not a mutt, he's an..." I began, but Harry shot me a look and I fell silent.

"He's trained in search and rescue. He's one of the best trackers around," Harry replied.

"Really?" Anderson looked at Wolf as if noticing him for the first time.

I patted Wolf's head, and Wolf wagged his tail.

* * *

We sat in the tiny conference room while Harry played back the tape from the crash site. The smashed buggy twisted into an almost unrecognizable form, but I recognized the wheels and a bit of the suspension. Long gouges ran through the metal. I winced. If Kevin was in it, he was toast.

"You can see the scratch marks alongside the metal," Harry was saying. "And if I play back thirteen-twenty-two-oh-five, you can see the tracks."

I leaned forward. Paw marks in the snow. Lots of them with claw indentations. Six-toed marks with generous pads, splayed to keep traction on the snow and ice. The video went too fast. "Can you back that up?" I said.

Harry clicked the repeat and slowed it down. "Looks wolfish."

Wolf pricked his ears at his name.

"Must be some hell of a wolf," Anderson said. "Those tracks measure a good fifteen centimeters across."

"Might not be as big as you think," I said absently and fell silent.

Harry cleared his throat.

I glanced at him. "Oh, the feet could snowshoe out for traction. That would give the animals greater stability in snow."

"Animals?" Anderson looked at me appraisingly.

"There are four distinct animals, as far as I can see." The room became very quiet. I looked from one man to the other. "What? We're going out to look for him, right? Wolf will find him."

"I'll have to notify Representative Allen that his son may be dead." Anderson scrolled through the tablet he had in his hands.

I formed the words with my mouth, but nothing came out. *That Allen?* I knew Kevin's last name was Allen, but I had no idea his father was the head of the NASA subcommittee in Congress. Damn. They'd pull the plug faster than you could say "Kepler-16b." But Kevin couldn't be dead. He just couldn't.

"Belay that," Harry said. "We don't know if he's dead."

"Four predators around a smashed hull of what's left of the buggy and you think he could still be alive?" Anderson shook his head. "Unlikely."

I felt sick. I felt responsible. Kevin was a kid—and I unwittingly let him go collect specimens on the western ridge. If he was dead...

I pushed that thought from my mind. "I'll find him."

"You're hardly search and rescue personnel," Anderson sneered.

"Maybe not, but Wolf is. And he only listens to me." I crossed my arms. "What do you say, Harry?"

My commander glanced at the lieutenant apologetically. "If there's any way we can find him, I suggest we try it."

* * *

My certainty that we would find Kevin was somewhat dampened when I learned that Anderson would be accompanying Wolf and me. Wolf could find Kevin, but I wasn't sure how Anderson would fit in. Wolf is particular about his humans, and it was obvious he wasn't fond of the lieutenant. Still, an extra pair of eyes and hands was helpful, even if they were attached to an asshole.

I could feel the sweat as my heat suit started working overtime again. Luckily it pulled the moisture away from my body, but it left me with a slightly clammy feeling. I wished once again for something a little less high tech like wool. Eyeing Anderson, I noted that he wasn't faring much better in his suit either and the sweat trickled from his brow. Great, we'd both look like prunes when this was over.

Lieutenant Anderson flew the hopper that would normally give us medium range. I ran the infrared, hoping to catch a glimpse of either Kevin or whatever predator it was that attacked the buggy. Nothing obvious showed up on the viewport except horned beasts and a couple of quadrupeds that I had classified earlier. They seemed indiscriminate in their feeding habits, thus earning them the ubiquitous title of omnivore. Their size precluded them from feeding on horned beasts, except as carrion.

We arrived at the buggy's site a little after nineteen hundred. The twin suns had already set, but Kepler-16b rose majestically above us, lighting the sky in an eerie twilight blue. The buggy was just as I had seen it from the drone pictures—a mangled, twisted ball of metal, composite, and plastic. I stepped out of the hopper and Wolf loped out, looking and sniffing eagerly. He knew Kevin. Nothing but the sharp, crisp air with something that smelled a bit like pine reached my nostrils.

"What is Laika doing?" Anderson asked as we followed Wolf. " He will be able to find Allen, won't he?"

"Yeah, he's good," I said, looking at the wreckage in front of us, my mouth dry. It looked worse than the drone footage. "Wolf will signal if he finds anything." I watched the dog as he snuffed the ground and the footprints, his hackles rising on his neck and back. Usually, he only did that in the presence of other canids. He paused and sat, looking at me meaningfully.

"He found something." I ran to him and took a look. Wolf sat next to a piece of the buggy where something dark had torn off. I reached for it.

"Don't!" Anderson snapped at me. Wolf growled.

I plucked the black fabric from the metal. "It's part of Kevin's heat suit." I pointed to the tracks that led away from the buggy. "The creatures went that way. If you look closely, you'll see their tracks overlay Kevin's footprints."

Anderson scowled and squinted at the tracks. "It looks like he's running." He finally spoke after a few minutes.

I shrugged. "The other tracks make it tough to conclude."

Anderson drew his sidearm—a compact projectile weapon capable of firing more than a hundred rounds. "Can your dog track them?"

Now it was my turn to frown. "What's that for?"

"If they're predators, they're dangerous." He saw my disgust on my expression. "Listen, doctor, I know I'd be plugging one of your valuable life forms, but it's a moot point trying to find Kevin Allen if it eats us."

I swallowed, but my mouth was dry and tasted like expired space rations. He had a point. I occasionally carried a weapon when going into unknown areas, but I never had to draw it. These creatures were after Kevin—I couldn't accept that they might have already killed him. I nodded and gave Wolf the command to find Kevin.

It was slow going. The snow reached up to my knees and made it hard to move. Wolf didn't bound ahead like he normally did; instead, he stayed a few meters ahead of us and followed the tracks. Truth was we really didn't need him— Kevin's and the creatures' tracks shone in the snow like a beacon. The lieutenant kept checking his device and nodded as Wolf led us into a forest of crystal needle trees. The tracks led into deep snow and then became confusing, crisscrossing everywhere with other tracks of what had to be either herbivores or omnivores.

Wolf's nose told him where to go. After sniffing the tracks for a few minutes, he must have sorted them out because he took a path deeper into the forest. For once I was glad to have Anderson there; the shadows deepened and threw us into an eerie twilight. I kept having the feeling that something or someone was following us and kept looking around, expecting to see creatures with sharp teeth gazing at me.

Wolf began to act nervous. I called him to me and put on a leash. I didn't need him bounding through the snow after shadows. I shivered as the temperatures plunged. I knew Kevin might not make it through the night since his heat suit was damaged. Hell, I might not, given how cold I was.

If the lieutenant was cold, he didn't show it. Instead, he entered something in his device and tapped it. He frowned at the readings.

"Something wrong?" I asked.

Anderson shook his head. "Weird anomalies. It shows some sort of life form winking in and out."

I hesitated. "May I see?" Wolf halted and circled back to us.

I took the scanner and stared at the readings winking on and off. "Is it broken?"

Anderson shook his head. "Ran self-diagnostic on it three times."

A life form winked on. It seemed quadruped about twice the size of Wolf—not good. It then disappeared on the scanner. "Maybe it has a way to camouflage itself..."

"What?" Anderson said.

"Your scanner works on heat signatures, right?"

He nodded.

"Suppose the critters can hide their heat signatures?" I looked down at the device. "I mean, the adaptation would make sense out here. The horned beasts have a special sense to detect even the slightest degree of heat—it enables them to find liquid water and plants they prefer. It might help them with predators."

"You think whatever's out there might be able to change their heat signature?"

"It might. Make for one hell of an adaptation." I paused. "Imagine the critter able to make its signature small enough to mimic something the horned beasts like?"

Anderson stared at the device and tapped a few numbers. "They breathe, yes?"

I nodded.

"Then, I'll focus on CO_2 emissions." He switched the device and began cursing. I glanced at the scanner. CO_2 scanning wasn't as accurate as heat signatures, but I got a good idea what we were up against. Twenty or more. We were surrounded.

Anderson raised his weapon.

A low rumble issued from Wolf's throat. I gripped his leash, my hands shaking. He pulled hard, almost unbalancing me in the deep snow. And then, I saw the predators.

Silent, ghostly blue, with thick fur-like covering, they looked like wolves on steroids. Their tiny ears kept the heat from escaping and thick fur shifted blue and gray with perfect camouflage for the forest. Their teeth shone white against their huge mouths and their feet were thick and heavily padded with claws that looked more like a bear's than a wolf's. One more pull and Wolf's leash snapped. "Wolf!" I shouted as I landed face first in the snow. Wolf ignored me and went to the predator.

Anderson pointed his weapon at the predator.

"Don't! You'll shoot Wolf!" I shouted.

Anderson hesitated as he saw the predator and Wolf sniff each other's backside. The predator had a thick bushy tail that rivaled Wolf's in luxuriousness. A quick sniff to the muzzle and Wolf licked the predator's mouth. I stared as I pulled myself up. The predator put a huge paw on Wolf's shoulder. Wolf dropped into a play bow.

"What are they doing?" Anderson asked.

"They're communicating." My mouth hung open in utmost surprise. "This is all friendly."

"Friendly?" Anderson didn't lower the weapon, but he didn't shoot either. Wolf leapt up and nipped at the predator. The predator yipped and leapt in the air. Suddenly the two creatures, Earth and Kepler were bounding along and playing like friends. The other predators came in, and I was able to see the striking patterns of blue and gray along their fur. They approached us cautiously.

"Stand still," I said to Anderson. "They're curious about us."

"Will they attack?" Anderson asked, and I could now see sweat on his brow, despite the dim light.

"I don't think so—as long as we do nothing aggressive."

One of the Kepler wolves—I couldn't help but think of them as wolves approached me and sniffed my hand. I kept my hand relaxed as the Kepler wolf gently nudged it. Coming up underhand, I tickled its chin. It hopped back and then crooned at me. I knelt down and held out my hand palm up. It sniffed the glove and the heat suit. It tried to nibble and I flicked my finger on its nose. It jumped back. I laughed.

I stood up. "I think we're okay." I turned to see the Malamute wrestling playfully with the Kepler wolf. "Hey Wolf! Where's Kevin?"

Wolf turned to me with a doggy grin. He bounded into the forest to the right. I followed Wolf and the Kepler wolf through some deep snow. Anderson followed me. It didn't take us long.

"Hey! Cinthia! Is that you?" I heard Kevin's voice above me. I took out my flashlight and shone it up a tree. Kevin sat in the tree, shivering.

"You can come down, it's all right."

"But those wolf things..."

"Kepler wolves," I said grinning. "Wolf made friends with them. They accept us as part of their pack."

Kevin slowly skittered down the tree. "My hands are frozen."

"Mine, too." I watched as he landed and almost toppled into the snow. "Sheesh, Kev, you had us worried."

"The predators are okay?" He glanced at the two that followed me. Wolf had assumed his place next to me.

Anderson joined us. "You're lucky we had the dog with us," he said. "These creatures are smart, but they don't speak our language. They speak Wolf's language." He shook his head. "I still don't understand why they accepted us."

"It's the company you keep," I said, rubbing Wolf's ears. To my surprise, the Kepler wolf nudged my hand for a quick rub. "I'm part of Wolf's pack. Wolf included you as part of his pack. As long as dogs accept us as companions, the Kepler wolves are likely to include us as not prey." I rubbed my arms. "Come on, let's get back to the station. I'm freezing and I've now got a new species to catalogue."

Anderson laughed and shook his head—the first time I had seen him smile. He led the way back, escorted by bounding alien wolves and unearthly howls.

Kepler-47

The binary star Kepler-47 consists of a star much like our sun and a very cool, lower mass star—thus making it an odd binary pair. Perhaps stranger still, this is the first binary star system discovered with two planets orbiting the central binary star. Kepler-47c is a cool but temperate world. Let's take a voyage to this outer planet courtesy of modern medicine. However, be carful what you dream, it may not be all that you had hoped for.

Kepler-47-A,B	Stellar Characteristics
Temperature	5636 / 3357 Kelvins
Mass	1.0 / 0.36 Solar masses
Radius	0.96 / 0.35 Solar radii
Visual magnitude	15
Distance from Earth	4890 Light years
Orbital Period	7.45 days

Kepler-47b	Planet Characteristics
Temperature	450 Kelvins
Mass	>40 Earth masses
Radius	3.0 Earth radii
Orbital Period	49.5 days
Distance from Star	0.30 AUs

Continued on next page.

Melinda Moore

Kepler-47c	Planet Characteristics
Temperature	220 Kelvins
Mass	>40 Earth masses
Radius	4.61 Earth radii
Orbital Period	303 days
Distance from Star	0.99 AUs

Kokyangwuti
Melinda Moore

The Fourth World: Mother Earth

Kokyangwuti lay on the surgery bed in the hangar with wires and tubes inserted through her wrinkles and into her nerves, connecting her to the front of a spaceship like a spider feeding on a bug a thousand times her size. Old men surrounded her, carrying trays of prayer sticks fashioned with feathers. Beyond them hundreds of men stood around the ship, placing prayer sticks below it as the men next to her placed the trays below her bed. The men lit pipes and blew smoke over her and by the ship. The haze reminded her of breaking away from Earth's atmosphere as she flew the shuttles between Earth and Mars back when she was young. Earth's government had retired her, but her people needed her for one final journey: a one-way trip for the Hopi.

She looked through the smoke at the nose of her ship—her new body: sleek and shiny with no flabby skin to remind her of her age. She heard the beep of the machine monitoring her pulse as it quickened with her anticipation. Her people had always been opposed to cyberization, but they didn't trust a robot to fly the millennia-long journey to the moon orbiting Kepler 47c. The moon was The Fifth World, and the gaseous giant next to it was Paalölöqangw, for that's where all the Water Serpents had fled in the wake of global warming. The big cities hoarded water, and their rain dances brought no clouds flying over the mesas as the Sun grew hotter in his old age and loneliness. But the Sun for The Fifth World had a mate as did Paalölöqangw—two suns, two planets. The moon was alone like her.

The doctor smiled down and asked if she was ready. He was young, but not a child. If she were being transferred into a female shell, she would've sought him out after the surgery, probably a common occurrence among the cyberized. He was saving her life; it was only natural to have a crush on him. She'd never wanted to die, never accepted the cycle of life as placidly as her people. Being the vessel to The Fifth World was an honor beyond her comprehension. She nodded her head to the doctor.

The men backed away, chanting and singing. Past them she heard the steps and jingles of the women dancing. The lights in the smoke looked like bright stars dimming as the singing crescendoed. Drugs flowed into her, and the ship tugged her. For a moment, her spirit protested and tried to float away from the ceremony, but the three chiefs from the three mesas shouted their song and pushed her soul into the waiting ship.

She was a mere speck in the system, but as the electricity shot through her, she expanded and filled the shell. Lights flipped on in succession like motion sensors detecting her presence. As if seeking a beacon, her soul dove into a heart in the middle of the ship, which was made of mechanics and organics. The heart expanded and contracted with a lugubrious beat, pulsing hormones and electricity through her new body. She would have to regrow the tissue for the heart several times over the course of the journey.

A niece entered the ship and said, "Kokyangwuti, do you live?"

Sudden knowledge of the ship's system overwhelmed her. As she continued to expand, she grasped one node and made it focus on finding the communications center. Scarcely a nanosecond later she replied, "Alive and ready for our mission."

The Journey: Sipapu

Kokyangwuti felt empty as she always did at the end of the hormone cycle. The stars twinkled, and the planets reflected forever like her journey. She selected the audio for the song they performed at her transfer ceremony, and her heartbeat quickened. Music wasn't something to be enjoyed through ones and zeros—it had to be heard, like a good story. She had filled her human conscious time, as she called her contemplative moments, with recordings of the storytellers of her people and other cultures. Creation stories fascinated her the most, and she had made a chart of all the similarities and differences: male and female being central to most of them.

Her heart continued to beat. The spiderish mechanical limbs and hands whirred around the room in preparation for the heart renewal. If she didn't complete it, the journey would end and the Hopis would never make it to The Fifth World. Had the journey been lonely for the Old Spider Woman who had led her people from The Third World to The Fourth? Had the people been in stasis, or had she been able to talk to them as they swam through the deep waters? Her hands grabbed the heart that was as large as a kiva and ripped it out of the plugs. All ship controls stopped and time itself seemed to slow until she shoved the new heart in place. Elation. Fresh hormones coursed through her. She was invincible—a goddess.

She searched her checklist of ship repairs that needed to be done and sent instructions to her mechanical limbs in the appropriate areas. Now it was time to check on her cargo. The core of her essence slipped through the ship and over the thousands of people in a chemically induced stasis. She had lost a few more, but the percentage was lower than expected. Still, it was always the elders who left, and she was worried there would be none by the time they arrived at The Fifth World. She broadcast drums and bells throughout the ship and sang the ceremony of last rites as she switched their chemical from one that preserved live bodies to one that preserved dead ones. She did a last sweep through the circuitry of the masses and stopped at the doctor who had transferred her: Cheveyo.

He was about to cycle into REM. What did he dream? She was connected to him like she was to all her people, but she didn't know their thoughts. Hopefully, their minds were blank except for the REM induced to keep them functioning. But they were connected. A node slipped off her soul, through the wires to Cheveyo and into his thoughts. At first there was emptiness, but then she saw him standing on top of the First Mesa in the ruins of Walpi. She needed an avatar: black hair blew behind her in the desert wind, leaving bare a young body with smooth, sun-kissed skin.

"Kokyangwuti?" he asked.

"How did you know?"

"I've felt you with me the whole trip. You've been a comfort during the loneliness."

Centuries of isolation had made her forget how to interact normally. Her thoughts in the ship skimmed through stories for appropriate responses. "You've been lonely? But you're asleep."

"For too long." He stepped to her and wrapped his arm around her waist, kissing her lips and neck. The intense love-making made her want to extend his REM, but she knew that was dangerous. All too soon, his mind dove back into the abyss of stasis, and her consciousness hovered over her heart once more. It beat with a rapidity she had never had, gradually slowing. Alone again. Suddenly she had a nagging feeling that drove her to the lab where she grew her new heart. Her hands separated some of the tissue chemicals and put it in a small container while other hands rummaged through the spare parts of the ship. She would be giving birth soon.

The Fifth World: Oraibi

Kokyangwuti's children clattered on the console before the screen that showed their new home. They were no bigger than a human foot and had bulbous mechanical black heads and bodies with small hearts beating inside. They were attached to her limbs, and each had eight limbs of their own to help their mother with tasks she didn't want to do anymore. Kokyangwuti watched as they clacked in excitement. The small inner planet's orbit brought it between its giant mate Paalölöqangw and the two suns. A storm in the blue atmosphere of Paalölöqangw boiled and erupted, sending a serpent of water whipping off Paalölöqangw and showering into the orbit of The Fifth World. One hundred sixty legs tapped and clicked in the ancient Morse Code language. They wanted to wake the humans. "No," said Kokyangwuti. "We must wait a little bit into the cycle."

After her dream with Cheveyo, she had entered the dreams of all her people, not to make love but to see their thoughts. The three chiefs often had a nightmare about Kokyangwuti's heart exploding when they unplugged it: she hadn't known they planned to end her life when they arrived. She had led them to their salvation and her demise. But the Fifth World had a surprise.

* * *

The three chiefs and Cheveyo stood before the screen, staring out onto a dry riverbed and red dirt all the way to the horizon. Hopi children ran races with Kokyangwuti's children under the atmospheric shield produced by the ship. Kokyangwuti had separated the children from her when they had gravity, and the Hopi children welcomed them as part of the adventure of the new world. The chiefs had been less enthusiastic. "Those are abominations, not children!" scolded the first chief. "You knew it was wrong to make them!"

The second chief interrupted. "The abominations are the least of our worries. What happened to the water? We can't make this world livable without water. All our data said there was plenty here."

"It's Kokyangwuti's fault," said the third chief. "She's already angered the Water Serpents with her children!"

The three chiefs continued to argue with no response from Kokyangwuti. She could wait for them to tire themselves, as she had already waited millennia. Cheveyo interested her the most. They hadn't spoken outside of the dream even though they'd landed seven days ago. He took his eyes away from the screen and placed his hand on one of her consoles. "I understand," he said. Loud rapid thumps issued from the heart room.

"What do you understand?" one of the chiefs asked.

"She knows you plan to kill her," said Cheveyo. "I have felt a sadness in her for a long time now. And obviously, you want to kill our children as well."

"Your children?" The chiefs gaped.

"What is your plan, Kokyangwuti?" asked Cheveyo.

Kokyangwuti lit all the lights in the ship in her pleasure. Cheveyo was on her side. "I know the secret of the water, but I will not share it until I have the word of the three chiefs that my children and I won't be killed."

The chiefs mumbled their agreement, but it was not enough.

"After the climate has been made suitable and the shelters secured, I wish human forms for my children and me."

The chiefs grumbled more but in the end agreed.

"You will fashion prayer sticks and place them in the dry riverbed. At the end of every day, the people will perform rain dances. At the end of the small sun's cycle, the Water Serpents will grant you water."

The chiefs bowed and left to gather the people together.

"What did our researchers miss?" asked Cheveyo, still touching her console.

"Where the water comes from. When Paalölöqangw's mate passes between Paalölöqangw and her suns, tidal forces fling water into orbit. The storm lasts a day and the river will flow for a time, but the atmosphere is too thin to keep the water for long."

They paused in silence, Kokyangwuti wishing she had touch sensors where his hand was. "You did it," he said. "You led us through the sipapu just as Old Spider Woman led us to the Fourth World. We can begin again."

"And our children will be wise," said Kokyangwuti, "and shamans and chiefs. And the Water Serpents will give us life."

About the Contributors

M.H. Bonham played a rocket scientist many moons ago sometime between the formation of the Earth and now. (Hey, it *is* rocket science!) After working as a software engineer for aerospace, telecom and other industries, she became a professional author writing nonfiction, science fiction, and fantasy. She is a multiple award-winning author of more than thirty books and hundreds of short pieces. Some of her past and present activities included sled dog racing, unofficial llama wrestling (she lost), mountain climbing, goat herding, horseback riding, She is the publisher of Sky Warrior Books, which explains why she has no time. She is best known for the fantasy books set in the world of the *Chi'lan* including Amazon kindle bestseller, *Prophecy of Swords*. Another Amazon bestseller of hers is *Howling Dead*, a cyberpunk werewolf novel.

Visit her website at www.skywarriorbooks.com.

Mike Brotherton is the author of the hard science fiction novels *Star Dragon* and *Spider Star* (Tor), editor of the online anthology *Diamonds in the Sky*, and an astronomy professor at the University of Wyoming. His speciality is quasars and other active galaxies. He's a graduate of the Clarion West workshop and founder of the Launch Pad Astronomy Workshop for Writers. He blogs at www.mikebrotherton.com.

J Alan Erwine is a science-fiction writer, editor, and game designer. He has sold more than 40 short stories to a variety of markets, as well as three short story collections, and three novels. He is the co-designer of the Ephemeris Science Fiction Role Playing Game and the creator of the Battle for Turtle Island RPG. He has edited for ProMart Writing Lab, Sam's Dot Publishing, and Nomadic Delirium Press, and he edits the magazines, *The Fifth Di...* and *The Martian Wave* for Nomadic Delirium Press. When not writing and such, J loves to spend time with his amazing wife, Rebecca, and their three lovely daughters, Eryn, Juliah, and Alexis.

Visit J online at: http://www.jalanerwine.com

Laura Givens is a Denver Based author and artist. Her art has graced the covers of numerous publishers' books and magazines. She has provided illustrations for Orson *Scott Card's Intergalactic Medicine Show, Jim Baen's Universe, Talebones, Science Fiction Trails and Tales of the Talisman*. Her work may be viewed at www.lauragivens-artist.com. In 2010 she naively decided she could probably write stories as good as many she had illustrated. She has sold works ranging from zombie stories to space operas. She was co-editor and contributor to *Six-Guns Straight From Hell*, a weird western anthology, and is art director for *Tales of the Talisman* magazine.

Carol Hightshoe is a former Deputy Sheriff whose current day job is with the Professional Bull Riders. She's a *Star Trek* fan who loves shooting and photography, as well as writing SF and Fantasy. Books 1-4 of her Chaos Reigns Saga are currently available from Double Dragon Publishing. She has also had short stories published in various magazines and anthologies. In addition to her day job and her writing she is the editor and publisher of two online magazines (*The Lorelei Signal* and *Sorcerus Signals*), a print magazine (*Mystic Signals*) and is a small press publisher (WolfSinger Publications).

Before moving to Colorado, Carol spent five years in the Netherlands, courtesy of her husband and the US Air Force—and was there during the Chernobyl incident and on stand-by for possible evacuation due to radiation levels. She is married and has one son. Carol also shares her house with a very spoiled yellow (white chocolate) Labrador Retriever named Ijs Beer.

Steve B. Howell received his PhD in astrophysics at the University of Amsterdam and is currently employed by NASA as the project scientist for the Kepler mission. With over 800 scientific publications spanning research on variable stars, instrumentation, spectroscopy, and exoplanets, he is pleased to have *A Kepler's Dozen* be his debut in the realm of science fiction. He has written or contributed to numerous scientific books, and his textbook on digital detectors (CCDs) is the standard in college classes around the world. A frequent speaker at scientific conferences and public forums, he enjoys sharing astronomy with both experts and lay people and still believes that Pluto is a planet. He lives in the San Francisco Bay area with his partner Sally and their dog Molecule (Molly). He enjoys scientific challenges, the great outdoors, vegetarian gourmet cooking, and playing blues music. He does not like TV, shopping malls, or mean people. Steve met Dave Summers while observing at Kitt Peak National Observatory.

Gene Mederos was born in Havana, Cuba and immigrated to the United States with his parents and sister at the age of two. Raised in Brooklyn and later moved with the family to Miami, where he graduated from the University of Miami with a Bachelor of Fine Arts degree in 1987.

Currently a filmmaker in beautiful and esoteric New Mexico, Gene has a few other stories in print, "Moons of Blood and Amber" in the *Tangle XY* anthology published by Blind Eye Books, "A Touch of Frost" in the *Space Horrors* anthology and "The Thirteens" in the *Space Battles* anthology, both published by Flying Pen Press.

His short sci-fi film *Intruder*, is currently making the rounds of film festivals and has played in LA and at the Boston Sci-Fi Fest and Con.

Visit http://www.facebook.com/gene.mederos for film, artwork and more.

Melinda Moore lives in Albuquerque, NM: The Land of Enchantment. Possessing a love of adventure, she has been a dancer, professional musician, music educator, recipe creator, parent and now published author. She gives away designer coffee on her blog as well as running a monthly writing contest based on photographs. Check out her current thoughts and all the goodies at www.enchantedspark.com.

Rick Novy lives in Scottsdale, Arizona. His education is technical, holding degrees in physics, mathematics, and engineering. Through his career, he has flown satellites, helped develop surgical implants, and worked with various integrated circuits and sensors. He is now a freelance writer and also teaches in the mathematics department at the local community college.

Rick started writing seriously in the summer of 2004. In 2005, he attended Orson Scott Card's Literary Boot Camp. Since that workshop, his fiction has appeared dozens of times in both online and print venues. His novels, *Neanderthal Swan Song*, *Rigel Kentaurus*, and *Fishpunk* are available at most major online retailers everywhere.

Learn more: www.ricknovy.com

Anna Paradox always wanted one of those science fiction author bios that lists many different occupations. So far, she's collected mint weeder, combine driver, crew boss, bookkeeper, waitress, tutor, bookseller, telephone support, website host, life coach, author, editor, and graduate assistant. With the support of her husband, and upon completing her new M.S. in Agricultural Economics, she expects to collect a few more. Economic analyst or construction worker might be good.

David Lee Summers is the author of seven novels and over sixty published short stories. His writing spans a wide range of the imaginative from science fiction to fantasy to horror. David's novels include *Owl Dance,* a wild west steampunk adventure, and *Vampires of the Scarlet Order*, which tells the story of a band of vampire mercenaries who fight evil. His short stories and poems have appeared in such magazines and anthologies as *Cemetery Dance, Realms of Fantasy, Human Tales, Six-Guns Straight From Hell,* and *Apocalypse 13*. In 2010, he was nominated for the Science Fiction Poetry Association's Rhysling Award and he currently serves as the SFPA's vice president. In addition to writing, David edits the quarterly science fiction and fantasy magazine *Tales of the Talisman* and has edited two science fiction anthologies, *Space Pirates* and *Space Horrors*. When not working with the written word, David operates telescopes at Kitt Peak National Observatory. Learn more about David at davidleesummers.com.

Doug Williams currently works as an Observing Associate and programmer at Kitt Peak National Observatory. He is currently putting the polishing touches on his first novel, *Nine Knots* to be published, hopefully later in 2013 or early in 2014.

Mike Wilson has been writing poetry and short fiction for a decade. Recent publishing credits include *Lyrical Iowa, Tales of the Talisman*, and *Blinking Cursor* anthology. He has two collections currently for sale on Amazon, *Future Property* and *Mirror Worlds*. A fan of science fiction all his life, he currently resides in Des Moines, Iowa.

Made in the USA
Charleston, SC
11 May 2013